GALLANTS OF THE OLD COURT

A Novel

Author's Illustration to *Gallants of the Old Court*

MATEIU I. CARAGIALE

GALLANTS OF THE OLD COURT

Translated from Romanian by Cristian Baciu

Front cover image: *At Oteteleşanu's Terrace* (1915) by Romanian painter Ştefan Dimitrescu (1886–1933).

Cover design: Leo Orman

www.eLiteratura.net
www.eLiteratura.com.ro

ISBN-13: 978-606-700-172-3 (eLiteratura)
ISBN-10: 606-700-172-1

9 786067 001723

[This book can also be acquired in Kindle format, via Amazon.com.
The Kindle format ISBN: 978-606-700-173-0.]

For more information about this book please write to info@eLiteratura.com.ro or info@ePublishers.info.

Mateiu I. Caragiale (1885–1936)

Que voulez-vous, nous sommes ici aux portes de l'Orient, où tout est pris à la légère ...[1]

---

1 What do you expect, we are here on the doorstep of the Orient, where things are taken the easy way... The words are attributed to Raymond Poincaré (French conservative statesman, five times Prime Minister and one term of office as President of the French Republic between 1913 and 1920), over a conflicted railway business between the Romanian government and a French company. During the lawsuit, Poincaré stood in defence of the French party.

CONTENTS

Welcoming the Gallants

... au tapis-franc nous étions réunis.[2]

L. Protat

The vow I had made to myself the very day before to return home early came out an absolute mess, as it wasn't until about noon the next day that it happened.

Sunken between the sheets, I took no notice of the night creeping in. I had completely failed to keep a tally of the time. Indeed I would have slept on like a log but for this letter bustling in, tugging at me to undersign for receipt. Now, if you try to wake me up all you get is a sullen, sulky, surly lump. No signing in, thank you. Just a grumpy grunt to drive them away.

I fell into a doze again, but it was hardly meant to last. That nuisance of a letter was back in no time, along with the sudden torturous glare of a lamp. The villain of a postman had deemed fit to sign on my behalf. Predictably, he had to go with no token of my gratitude for it.

---

2 ...at the bistro we flocked together. The quote is supposedly assigned to L. Protat, an obscure early 20th century French pornographer.

I hate letters. The only bright news a letter has ever brought me was from my good old friend Uhry once. I do loathe letters. At that time, I used to burn them as they came.

The newcomer had little better to expect. A glimpse of the handwriting gave me a fair guess of the content. I was, by now, fed up with that home-made bland mash of counsel and reproof I was being served regularly with every beginning month—counsel to engage with manly drive on an earnest working course, and reproof for steadily failing to do so. It ended with the inevitable wish that God might hold me in His protection and all.

Amen to that! My pitiful condition was enough argument against any progress on any kind of course. As it was, I hardly managed to stir in my bed. My limbs disjointed, the small of my back dismantled, I felt like jelly. For a scary moment, my hazy mind invited the dire picture of apoplexy.

Well, no—not that far. But I'd gone far enough though: for a good month's time, silently and breathlessly, thoroughly and intently, I had been drifting away in drinking, philandering, and gambling. The past few years had amassed a host of vicious waves that tossed my frail lifeboat about, trying me almost beyond stretch. Poor in my defences, I ended up in utter disgust and a lust for forgetfulness in the foul way of the flesh.

The trouble was I'd made a headlong dash for it and felt I would soon have to admit defeat. In any case, my state of supreme exhaustion that night was less than could have snatched me out of bed, had even a fire broken out in the house. At least, that was how I felt.

And yet—there I was, all of a sudden, upright in the dead centre of the room, gaping in apprehension at the clock, with an abrupt memory of Pantazi expecting me for dinner. How fortunate indeed, to have been intruded upon by this family letter I now glimpsed in grateful acknowledgement. To think I could have missed an appointment with my most precious friend!

I got dressed and went out against weepy weather, remindful of winter setting in. There had been no rain to account for the overall pervasive dampness: eaves and leafless branches dripping, thick cold sweaty beads trickling down tree trunks and railings. The most inspirational weather for a drinking spree. The sight of rare amblers, like spectral illusions in the misty air, most of whom swaying in liquorous perplexity. Out of a tavern and down the steps came a lanky figure and collapsed to rest in a shapeless lump. I looked away in disgust.

The meeting place for that night was a far-off bistro, all the way to Covaci[3], so I hired a cab. It proved a wise choice, as I found the other invitees upon the second round of brandy, and our entertainer already on the third. I showed surprise at their early advent, but Pantazi explained he had come straight from home, while Paşadia and Pirgu had taken the shortest route from the "club", and what with the weather being too nasty to dally over appetisers…

---

3 One of several most popular streets in 19th-early 20th down-town Bucharest; the cobbles and walls of Covaci St. could spin a rich yarn of romance, dejection and mystery. A must-see for visitors, Covaci has been restored to preserve at least some of the flavour of its days of local glory.

Pantazi ordered another round of brandies. The cheers we muttered while clinking glasses sounded desperately cheerless. I feared I might doze off again. Compared with the vulgar merchants' party nearby, which was gaining steam— after all, it was Saturday—our table looked rather like a funeral feast.

The borscht, properly served with sour cream and green peppers, was downed in sullen silence, all eyes glued to the bowls. Pirgu, in particular, seemed to be consumed by gloomy thoughts. I was preparing to engage some conversation gambit when the fiddlers started on a waltz for which I knew Pantazi had a soft spot. It was a slow, sensual, sad flow, almost funereal in its tones; a languid sway that carried a wavering, wistful, infinitely woeful key to leave a dolorous mark on any listening ear. The rumour in the room fell into dead silence as the deep magic of the melody went gliding across the bridged cords of the fiddles. Sinking to a lingering lower timbre, gently subdued to the sound of painful tenderness and chagrin, the music overflowed with wistful redolence of agonising fantasy.

Pantazi wiped his teary eyes.

'Ah!' said Pirgu to Paşadia with a suave look and a silky voice, 'this is the music I'll have them play as I usher you to your eternal resting place. A rare treat to season the prime of my life—how graceful, how radiant, how ravishing! I hope you won't let me lay in waiting too long for it, will you... And there I am, yours truly, basted in wine, and master Pantazi by my side, me bidding such a heart-rending farewell of my irreplaceably lost friend that the audience can't hold back the scalding tears pouring down their melancholy-ridden cheeks...'

Paşadia remained silent.

'Oh yes,' Pirgu purred on, 'to think of the splendour of it all! I'll be the one to carry your accolades resting on a velvet cushion. And then, when they dig you out seven years on for funeral office, I'll bet they'll see the same neat, spruce, pompous figure, not a single white hair on your crown, embalmed in quicksilver and spirit like a bell pepper in salt and vinegar...'

Riding on stray thoughts, Paşadia lent him no ear, and my deep disdain for Pirgu made me hate to see him get away with it.

Left to my own devices in Bucharest at a fairly young age, I had tried to refrain from random acquaintances. In fact, I had carefully selected my company, and Gorică Pirgu would have never been part of it, had it not been for his close companionship with Paşadia, to whom I looked up in supreme reverence.

Paşadia—a morning star, no less. Some strange quirk of nature had bestowed on him one of the most exquisite frames a human brain has ever been blessed with. As chance would have it, I've met with many of those who are looked upon as the country's elite, but few were they who could boast such a rich collection of wonderfully balanced virtues as this underdog of fate, who had wilfully lent himself to public oblivion. And there is no other, to the best of my knowledge, who might have invited so much vicious rancour from his own kind.

This, I had heard, he owed to his appearance, in part. But then, what a stately head! Some passionate, disquieting daemon seemed to slumber within, given away by the features of his weathered face, lips pursed in frozen disillusionment, flared nostrils and a hazy viscous look slithering between heavy eyelids. His voice, little more than a muffled drawl, sounded weary with sullen disgust.

His life, of which he rarely deigned to disclose a piece, had been a full record of bitter struggle. Born to parents of a certain influence and wealth, he was given to be raised among strangers and then dispatched for studies abroad. Upon return, all he met with was implacable hostility, rejection and betrayal. Little was left but had been plotted against him. His works, the sacrificial offering of his youth, had been confronted with fierce, as it was unjust, criticism while everybody was striving to silence him down. At the end of many a bleak year strewn with dire ordeals enough to crush a giant, Paşadia had come out in callous armour. Far from a submissive character, his self-possession and fortitude had sailed him safely through the darkest moments. While relentlessly following his path, he had managed to turn even the direst of circumstances to his own advantage. With unrivalled patience and endurance he had lain waiting for his lucky strike, grabbed it as it came and squeezed his rightful due out of it. At the end of a lot of trouble, once he made his mark he indulged in ruthless, as it was perversely delicate, retaliation; he could freely have his fling now, sending ripples of perplexed confusion and awe through the round of his former detractors; the path to fame and glory was finally smoothed out for him. At this point, when he could reach out for anything and have it, he stepped back. To my mind he might have taken this decision, if only in part, in self-awareness of his own passionate nature: he might indeed have been afraid of his darker side, of the murky daemons that occasionally managed a cynical stab through his icy social shield. A grain of granted power added to the poison piled up in his calloused heart would have sparked disaster. For he trusted nothing like virtue, honesty, goodness, and had no mercy or compassion for human weaknesses, to which he appeared to be a perfect stranger.

His stepping down from politics was less of a surprise than the abrupt turnabout in his lifestyle. At an age when others would rather settle down in compunction, Paşadia—until then, a living example of moderation—suddenly plunged into reckless debauchery. Did he do it in careless, defiant exhibition of hitherto hidden practices? Or was it the outburst of what was bred in the bone, for too many long years stifled by his hunger for success? For it is hard to reasonably expect of anyone to have leapt overnight from the lamb's fleece into the wolf's hide. Rarely had I met a gambler of such lofty, majestic appearance, a more dedicated philanderer, or a more distinguished drinker. And yet, there was not the least trace of the classic degenerate about him: soberly elegant, of rare distinction in garb and gab, he remained the same perfectly western-looking man of the world, from top to toe. No one could have been better qualified to chair a High Assembly or an Academy. One could hardly relate the stately figure sauntering in erect dignity on his evening promenade, closely followed by the cabby dutifully bridling his horse at idling pace, to the sordid, sleazy establishments in which this impeccable gentleman would bury himself through the deep of the night. This man's life story confounded me greatly, as I sensed it was driven by some intense spiritual torment of impenetrable mystery.

If I have indulged in a fairly lavish portrayal, it is only to conjure up once more the figure of this noble character, whose memory I hold in high regard. For I must confess to the rare privilege of having also known a very different Paşadia, in stark contrast to the night rambler through the round of the most infamous of Bucharest's joints. I used to meet this alternate avatar at a no less unconventional station.

A God-forsaken back alley not far from Mogoşoaia Bridge[4] led to a shadowy unkempt garden that embraced an old, bleak, inhospitable-looking house in which even the most remote nook breathed a reflection of the landlord's stern humour. I would find him there in his study, a place of privacy inviting to introspection, a tight refuge against the world. The room was a display of timber-coloured wall cloth, walled-in wardrobes and cases, and heavily curtained windows. I lost count of the hours I spent there, riveted in the large armchair by the host's fascinating discourse—a perfect marriage of deep sense and balanced, elevated style which arrested the auditor's attention in silky magic chains. But Paşadia was also an accomplished wordsmith on paper, for many masterful pieces had come from under his pen in his younger years. He was incredibly widely read. No one had I met with a better command of history, the study of which had nourished and polished his innate genius of a flawless judge

---

4 What is known today as Calea Victoriei (Victoria Avenue) in central Bucharest used to be called Podul Mogoşoaiei (Mogoşoaia Bridge) because it was originally (1692) paved with wood.

of character. He relished in foretelling the nearing miserable downfall to this or that notable who were at the peak of their career, and I will never forget the cynical glint in his eyes as the ominous words came out.

Paşadia Măgureanu! His affection for me was like a gift from Holy Providence, and I am proud to have been a disciple of this illustrious, adamant rebel. Of all the faults and flaws the mob would hang to his effigy, I could only consent to one: his indulgence of Gorică. Indeed, I couldn't forgive him that.

Gore Pirgu was the ultimate rascal. His silly ludicrous antics, remindful of an impudent jester, had gained him the reputation of a smart fellow, doubled by that of a jolly good fellow—which was indeed amazing, for all he was really good at was gleeful offense and mischief. This devilish off-spring's heart hosted an amalgam of a dog catcher and a grave digger. Corrupt to the bone from early age, addicted to pilfering and coin pitching, later wallowing in lechery with the maidservants, prowling about in the company of pimps and swindlers, he had been the Benjamin of Cazes Coffee House and the Cherub of call houses. I felt disgust at the thought of probing further into the deplorable nature of this morbid individual who had a singular attraction to whatever was tainted by squalor and decay. Pirgu had it in his blood to plunge into such gipsy-like depravity as was once common in these parts, with sordid suburban love affairs, wining and dining sprees at monasteries, with vulgar, infamous songs to crown the spectacle of gross decadence. The scope of his conversation narrowed round card playing—his sole voca-tional aptitude, in fact—and the venereal diseases that had prematurely withered his vigour. These gambits he spiced with the kind of humour that charmed the sort of audience who valued his imbecility. Amazingly, this was the character Paşadia had deemed fit to abide in his orbit while openly despising him and never missing an opportunity to ruthlessly snub him.

'Would you please attend to your companion,' he said to me, 'he seems to be having a suicidal impulse—there, he's all but gulping down his knife!'

Indeed, Gorică would work the knife fiercely into the boiled sterlet before him, then roll the morsel in the mayonnaise sauce and, still with the knife, thrust it deep into his mouth. I played deaf to the remark and blind to the scene. Pantazi bent down, as if fumbling for something under the table.

'Among the most elementary precepts of social etiquette,' Paşadia went on, 'one can read: no knife for vegetables and fish, no fork for cheeses, and by no means knife to mouth. But—well, this is for the chosen few, for royalty and nobility; boorish commoners are spared, I should say. You can't have swine drink out of goblets, can you.'

There could be no deadlier insult for Pirgu, who thought of himself as a virtuoso of social graces. He recollected himself hastily, cocked his head up and retorted in pathetic redress:

'Spare me your lofty fancies, will you—unless you want me to change my tune. Old age has twisted your mind, it seems...'

In pursuit of conciliation, Pantazi called for the champagne to be served—which, following our convivial tradition, was poured into large glasses. Pirgu said when to a trifle finger depth, on top of which he splashed a pint of light soda water. Of the four of us, his drinking defences were the poorest. You might say he mostly pretended to be drinking, while drowning his belly in light wine and soda—for which he would invariably ask for a blue siphon seltzer bottle. Against all odds, however, he seldom happened to be sober in the morning; and when he was tipsy he would go about playing such pranks on people as would make a man of some decency stay away from the public eye forever.

Upon a collective toast to Pantazi, our dearly beloved entertainer, we took a sip of the delightfully invigorating wine. Pirgu barely moistened his lips and his face twisted in a wry grimace.

'Champagne and no lass will taste like rain,' he mumbled.

Our club protocol expressly ruled out the female side from our dining parties, with no exception to be ever admitted. Several times Gorică had ventured to be indulged to invite one or two ladies of his private companionship, and Pantazi would have fain followed, but Paşadia had remained in adamant opposition. So, we were left to furtive cocky glances to the dames sitting at neighbouring tables, who would, more often than not, readily respond with sly lascivious squints.

Paşadia's hazy, sulky gaze proceeded to peel a well-rounded Jewish lady of her apparel. I followed suit in this honourable occupation, well assured that my distinguished friend would take no offence. Straight opposite him, her table was a little farther off. A cold gleam in her dark velvet eyes between silky lashes against a pale marble face, she was well aware of her resplendent oriental beauty in full bloom and offered a sight of august immobility—a kosher descendant of the chosen race. Haughtily impassive she looked, and so must have looked her great-great-great grandmothers while fiendishly denuded and dragged to the slave market, or later savagely stretched on Torquemada's windlass. As she was sitting with her legs crossed, her dress had come knee-high, exposing a pair of flawlessly chiselled shanks through the subtle transparency of black stockings. When she decided to cover her legs, she did so with a nonchalant gesture and without blushing.

Pirgu was shamelessly staring at a classic tradeswoman flaunting her gaudy garb, a copious display of paint and powder barely accomplishing to hide her red, sunburnt cheeks. Beaming languorously at her, eyes half closed, he raised his glass, took a delicate sip, then licked his lips with delight.

Pantazi was the only one to take no notice around. His usual melancholy gaze, dreamily benign, was floating weightlessly ahead. He beckoned for more champagne.

In the meantime, Pirgu was going overboard with his antics. Holding his empty glass to his eye as a comically improvised telescope, he was blowing kisses with his other hand to the handsome saleslady who was laughing her head off in copious reward. Paşadia cautioned him to compose himself, or he might see trouble coming his way.

'What a sight you would make,' he said, 'to be dragged out and kicked in the back!'

Pirgu gave him a derisive glance:

'Think I'm one of your kind, to be shoved away like a poor old rascal? Think there's anyone doesn't know me here or wherever? Think there's a place around I wouldn't hang my hat like home?'

To prove his words, he stood up and made a show of sauntering over to the tradeswoman, bowing to kiss her hand and whispering something into her ear; then he passed through the round of the other tables. Purposely, he dallied awhile with the shapely Jewish lady.

'You know,' he said as he finally came back, 'Raşelica[5] was wondering, why would a man of most genteel manners and noble descent like me abide such uncouth companionship? Downright furious she was. Told her to let it pass; told her one's a sorry old pervert—used to make some ripples in his good old days, but now's just a pitiful dotard; and the other has yet to come of age...'

Paşadia swallowed hard and kept his words at bay. I followed in his wake. And yet, I could hardly make a secret of my bewilderment at Pirgu's amazing social scope.

There were people from all walks of life, hosts of them—nay, all of them, for all I knew... Indeed, I was wondering if there was a soul he didn't know, or a door but would open for him. The heavily bolted sanctuaries of suspi-

---

5 A diminutive for Raşela (Rachel).

cious traders, the impenetrable citadel of the affluent Jewish caste, the infamous dens of degenerate upstarts would all open their gates wide for Gorică—or at least the back door, sometimes. It was amazing how he never inspired the faintest trace of repulsion or apprehension, how everybody refused to discern, behind the roguish sycophant, the essential fiendish beast in dedicated service of evil fate. As a matter of fact, he didn't as much as try to conceal his depravity—on the contrary, he would boast of such infamous exploits as would have been listed for legal custody behind the bars, if not in a madhouse.

As far back as his school years, he would introduce his friends to diseased prostitutes. With immoderate diabolical imagination, he engaged body and soul in inciting to promiscuous overindulgence, as if it were the ultimate mission of his life. His artful schemes in all sorts of dubious affairs had brought a few prodigal sons to ruin and several women to depravity, and many a respectable name owed him their fall to shameful disgrace. If there was some nefarious plot being played around, Gorică must have had his share in it; and this was only due to his crude, insatiable appetite for mischief and derision, in the service of which he would spare none of his Mephistophelian resourcefulness. From snooping around to defamation, to gossiping, to breeding discord, to denunciation, to blackmail, to anonymous threats—anything would do to serve his vile case. The question rose: what more was needed to range Gogu Pirgu with the jolly bad fellows?

Flattered at what he took for a compliment, he didn't need me to ask him twice to start recounting the last adventure of Mrs Mole, only to be soon disrupted by Raşelica's departure. With a smooth lithe gait, she came past our table to pick her cloak off a nearby hook. Pirgu leapt to his feet to offer assistance. Perfectly carved in the female pattern she was, the notion of a dark tropical flower, overflowing with the sweet poisonous perfume her every move would radiate to fill the air with consuming passion. At close quarters, however, without losing a touch of her resplendent beauty, there was something forbidding about her fibre: more than in other women you could feel the archetypal fiendish Eve, forever implacable, forever bearing temptation and death. As her dispassionate glance swept over our corner, there was a cruel spark as it crossed Paşadia's flimsy gaze.

A somewhat lanky youngster followed in her step, his back humped, dark rings round his eyes, his cheeks an unhealthy feverish scarlet. A vicious dry cough shook his frail frame relentlessly. He gave Pirgu a faint good-bye smile, as if in painful foreknowledge of it being the last time they met.

'That's Mişu,' Pirgu whispered to us. 'He's on the hearse, as good as gone. The second beau she's bringing down in just three years—let aside what game she's been chipping in accessory frolic. Hell of a woman, I tell you...' Then, turning to Paşadia: 'And so you want to take a crack at her, don't you? Think you got the right kind of shoes for that? Well then, just say the word and let me put you in, it's all in my line, you know...'

Ignoring him, Paşadia leisurely dried down his glass. Pirgu insisted:

'Why dilly-dally, old man? The diggers are waiting for you anyway, bells ringing and all. Everybody knows you've been long dragging on liquorice and purgatives, only to see another day. Now, since you're at the gate, why not make a glorious passage, at least?...'

In the meantime, the bistro had come alive with a bustle of guests leaving their seats and hurrying to the door. The firefighters' coaches were hurtling past, blaring their horns. The garcon waiting on us said it was nothing to worry about: a chimney had caught fire near the Old Princely Court Church, but they had already managed to put it out before the firemen arrived. Some of the guests, who either owned or rented in the vicinity, were fretting at the ugly thought of the fire spreading and reaching their abode in a place so crammed with buildings shabbily leaning against one-another.

Our conversation veered round to the Old Court— which, in the absence of the green-steepled church bearing its name, would have sunk into perfect oblivion. With distinguished competence, Paşadia gave us a display of nearly all he knew about those age-old princely precincts. Not much to marvel at, it seemed. Like the rest of the town, the Court had more than once risen from ashes, and it must have covered quite a stretch, judging by the vaulted ruins to be found beneath much of the neighbourhood—even under this our bistro, in fact. The overall design of the Court was not hard to imagine, as it largely followed the monasterial pattern, with building clusters to accommodate a host of commoners and gypsies. No regular architecture, no particular style—it all added up to a grotesque assortment of patched and bungled masonry to expose the horrid hind stage of a heinous sovereign clique, an amalgam of outlandish degenerate villains copiously adulterated with gypsy blood.

I asked him why, to his mind, our people had failed to follow in the Western path of accomplishing grand and sublime in memory of ages to come. Was it not for the debility of our line of sovereigns, and our fatalistic fear of the next invasion? After all, the noble motive of raising stately edifices did not fail some of our voivodes—Brâncoveanu[6], for one, had left behind many an opulent court and mansion. No, he said; an artistic penchant was an exclusive privilege of peoples of distinguished descent, and ours was not the case, since we had contributed nothing to the treasury of civilisation. With that, he fiercely fell upon Brâncoveanu's memory and shoved the voivodal fur cap off his head, then the Holy Empire princely bonnet, then the Hungarian count's coronet, finally snatched his collar of the Russian Order of St. Andrew the First-Called and went on to smear the voivode's portrait in the likeness of a sly Bulibaşa[7], a menial hypocrite, born only to bow low.

True, in the line of the mighty lords of his time, he fell for the same feverish fervour: to build, to seed, to adorn—but what's left behind this wretched, rotten, rich ras-

---

6 Constantin Brâncoveanu was Voivode of Wallachia between 1688 and 1714. Rather ambiguous in foreign policy, he was torn between the tides of the Ottoman and the Russian Empires (see Russo-Turkish War, 1710/1711), which is why he was beheaded by the Turkish sultan as a "traitor". He was, however, a great patron of culture. During his rule, a number of Romanian, Greek, Slavonic, Arabic, Turkish, and Georgian texts were printed with the aid of a printing press planted in Bucharest, and an original architectural style synthesising Renaissance and Byzantine architecture took shape in Wallachia, to be later known as the "Brâncovenesc style" (a sort of Romanian Renaissance), in memory of its initiator.

7 Bulibasha: a gypsy king or leader of a gypsy community.

cal who reigned in the prime of Baroque splendour? Indeed, what did he leave behind? The pillars of Hurez[8]? The porch of Mogoşoaia[9]? Potlogi[10]? What?... How can we possibly boast of such ridiculous ancestry as this pathetic effigy, this irresolute cheat?! To save us from shame, all memory should be cleared of such hopeless impostors!

Paşadia's outburst was of little surprise to us. Bitterly prejudiced against anything that bore the Romanian mark, he could often boil over with wanton criticism. At such moments, the grim ball of hatred lurking deep within would flare up in a devastating surge, driving him into blind battle with all claws and fists. On the other hand, his argument did hold a certain shade of truth, and that kept me from standing in resolute defence of that slice of history—which had however, in earlier years, inspired my hand to adorn an iconostasis with beautiful icons, in almost pious fervour. In any case, my would-be advocacy would have proved futile, since Paşadia was not late to confess to better thoughts:

'Funny though—to my taste, the art of these humble vestiges doesn't live up to as much as their historic worth— and yet, I can't deny them a certain quality of discreet seduction. My fantasy somehow flies free and I feel moved, deeply moved, even before the cheapest of these relics...'

---

8 Hurezi Monastery, a post-Byzantine architectural blend in Vâlcea county, Southern Romania, built by C. Brâncoveanu.

9 Mogoşoaia Palace, a combination of Venetian and Ottoman elements, nearly 10 kms from Bucharest, built by C. Brâncoveanu.

10 Potlogi Palace, 45 km from Bucharest, built by C. Brâncoveanu.

'Well, you have my deep sympathy,' said Pirgu, 'for you yourself are a venerable ruin—though not quite well preserved, I should say.'

There was laughter round the table. And that was how we would idle the hours away. For the last month the cult of Comus[11] had brought us together, almost daily, over either lunch or dinner.

Our true delight, however, came from the long, warm conversations turning from travelling to arts, to letters, to history—history was indeed a subject of our particular fondness. But the lofty academic distinction of those dissertations was occasionally smeared by Pirgu's crude humour, only to spoil our peaceful bliss. The company of this deplorable character who stood in fiendish ignorance of the written word was often dispiriting. Fortunately, Paşadia was richly rewarded with the presence of Pantazi, a crystal-clear mind and an advised free spirit. Their colloquy was a fascinating display of knowledge and views of which I was eager to digest every single word. The notes I took of those colloquiums are enough consolation and compensation for all material loss I've suffered since the war.

To my bitter annoyance, we couldn't linger on that soiree to our hearts' content, as Paşadia was due off to some mountain resort, sometime around midnight.

'I shall be looking forward to seeing you again at my place, on my return,' he said. Then, to Pirgu: 'How about a

---

11 Comus (Komos) is a god of Greek mythology, presiding over nocturnal feasts; son of Bacchus and following in the same orgiastic line, Comus stands for excess, chaos, anarchy.

few poker rounds on that occasion? A fair chance for you to get the hang of the game.'

This was more than Pirgu could take. He blew off in a surge of the most profane collection of invectives, the kind you could hear from cab drivers to market mongers to petty servants. And so we learned that, before dinner, Paşadia and Pirgu had run a fiendish encounter at the gambling house, where Pirgu ended up flat broke as he was cleared of twenty-five twenties, plus as much in debt.

To calm him down, Pantazi offered to lend him some money. Pirgu declined in self-sufficient arrogance and, to our amazement, produced a bulky envelope packed with one-hundred notes. He had made it over a night-long gamble of *chemin-de-fer* at a private home, the Arnoteanus'. Paşadia asked his due, but Pirgu spurned him outright:

'Oh no, not that!'

Pantazi paid the bill and topped it with fat tips for the waiters and the fiddlers. And so, we left. As we came out into the narrow lane outside the bistro, where a hackney coach was waiting for Paşadia, we ran into a bundle of people tumbling our way, laughing and screaming their guts out. At the heart of the melee, roaring like a wild beast, a woman was fiercely struggling against three stout gendarmes[12] who could hardly hold her in place. The four of us took a step backwards as she got so close as almost collapsed in our arms.

---

12 Gendarmes: a branch of the police force in Romania and some other European countries (France, for instance).

The woman was helplessly inebriated. Old and withered, her head kerchief hanging loose, all dressed in rags, with one foot bare, and what with her paroxysmal rage, she looked very much like an apparition from hell. There were streaks of vomit down her tattered clothes, which were also wet below the waist. The dire picture electrified an ebullient party of street rascals and harlots who were tailing after her in a grotesque cortège, calling out: 'Pena! Pena Corcoduşa!'[13]

I noticed Pantazi start at the name and suddenly grow pale. At the sight of the four of us, Corcoduşa ran into a fit of blind fury and spewed such a tirade as would have dismayed even the most callous of hearts. Pirgu himself was left dumbfounded.

'Listen carefully and take notes,' Paşadia whispered to him, 'it's a rare chance to add up to your basic education.'

The gendarmes dragged the drunken woman halfway down the bridge, where she dumped herself down like a bear, doggedly refusing to be helped up. Pantazi approached a little girl in the crowd whose bright, confident, smiling eyes were glued to that scene of ultimate human degradation, and asked her if she had any knowledge of the wretched woman.

'She's Pena Corcoduşa,' the girl said. 'Got drunk again. Quite nice when she's sober, but blows her top off when she gets pissed.'

---

13 Corcoduşa, pronounced [korko'dusha], is a nickname (the feminine adaptation of wax cherry or plumcot).

Pantazi slipped a few farthings in the girl's hand to make her tell more. And so we learned that Pena lived somewhere near the Old Court, that she would serve round the church candle shop, sometimes did odd jobs at the market place, and was often called on to wash a corpse for burial. She was also known to have spent some time in a madhouse, in earlier days...

The gendarmes took great pains to heave the woman up. As she felt her feet firm on the ground and her eyes fell on us again she bristled with anger, ready to resume her welcoming charge. Brutally jerked by the men, her voice faded in stutters as she choked on the words. However, she somehow managed to cry out after us:

'Hey there, you gallants!... You Ol' Court gallants!'

Could it be that some restless spirit of olden times had spoken in her voice? For it seemed as if little in the world would have been more pleasurable to Pantazi's ear than this long-forgotten, outmoded turn of phrase. His face lit with delight as he kept echoing it over and over again.

'Indeed, you could hardly find more inspired wording,' Paşadia admitted. 'It beats the Rakes of the Bronze Horse, equally notorious back in Louis XIII's days[14]. It's got a chivalrous note to it, a shade of magic. An excellent title for a book it would make.'

---

14 Reference is made to a notorious meeting place of infamous people in Paris, France, during the reign of Louis XIII. The place used to be marked by a bronze statue of a horse.

'Oh, you miserable Pena,' Pantazi murmured in a melancholy mood, after a moment of silence. 'Poor creature, I've never thought I'd see you again… Oh, for the memories you bring to my mind!'

'Why, d'you know her?' Pirgu asked in amazement.

'Oh, yes. It's an old story, an exotic romance, back in the Seventy-Seven War[15]. I don't think our women—women of all walks of life, I mean—have lost memory of the Russians' advent. Straight pandemonium it was. On plain straw mats or under lush canopies, a shower of rubles rained down on covetous Danaës[16]. The Russians had found Bucharest to be a convenient copy of ancient Capua[17]. Russian officers were a magnet for the dames' eyes. But the supreme idol every skirt was besotted with was handsome Sergej Leuchtenberg-Beauharnais, the emperor's grandson. Him they desperately trailed, in vain expectation to see him drop

15 The 1877 War between the Ottoman and the Russian Empires, where Romania sided with the Russians, consistently contributing to the Ottomans' defeat, and seized the opportunity to declare its national independence, readily acknowledged internationally. At the time, Romania still only consisted of Moldova and Wallachia, later to be completed with Transylvania at the end of World War I, in 1918.

16 In Greek mythology Danaë was princess of Argos, daughter of King Akrisios of Argos and mother of Perseus, whom she bore through intercourse with Zeus disguised as a shower of gold.

17 A city in today's western Italy, ancient Capua was a potential rival of Rome and Carthage in the 3rd c. B.C. Peacefully conquered by Hannibal, the Carthaginian general, the opulent city allegedly became a trap for his troops who became soft and demoralized by luxurious living — hence the disreputable connotation of the city's name.

his handkerchief. For it so happened that, from the very first night, he fell in the arms of a common woman, never to escape. She belonged in the slums; not very young either, judging by the stray grey hairs at the temples. I used to see her at fancy-dress balls or open-air cafés. Usually of a sullen disposition, she looked more strange than beautiful; actually, her charm came from her eyes—large, misty green eyes, fish-offal green as we call it around here, with a somewhat hazy look but neatly guarded by long lashes and shapely brows. Could it be that the prince's heart had fallen for a less common kind of magic? Well, maybe… Whatever the case, a ravishing passion entangled the slum-flower and the Prince Charming whose avatar garnered the glory of two imperial crowns. It was decided that after the war Pena would follow her lord and master to Russia, but Leuchtenberg went to die in the Balkans like a crusader. I joined the escort of his hearse up to the Prut[18]. On the evening of October the 19th, 1877, the mortuary train made a short stop in Bucharest, to receive the honours. The mortuary carriage looked like a true lit-up chapel where, against a profusion of burning torches and candles, several priests in ceremonial attire and cavalier guards in shiny armour were standing watch over the hero's hearse buried under an opulence of flowers. A shrilling scream broke the silence and a woman collapsed somewhere in the attending crowd. Now you know who she was. When she came to her senses, they had to tie her up. That was thirty-three years ago.'

Pantazi tapped his cigarette to drop the ash. The miserable story of Pena Corcoduşa was no less gratifying to us

---

18 The Prut River made the Romanian eastern frontier in 1877, as it does today.

than her juicy affront had been to him. Paşadia got on to his hired coach and bid us farewell.

'Good riddance!' was all Pirgu could think of calling out to him.

Staggering on his feet and stumbling on his words, Gorică had some difficulty telling us that old Mr. Poker in the flesh would have envied his masterful play.

'And yet he somehow got me in the ditch,' he whimpered, 'and I can't find solace till I've shaven this old mule clear of his last farthing...'

He insisted that we join him on a further pursuit:

'Come gentlemen, you won't regret it. Why, would I ever take you to some wretched vile dump?'

We asked him where that was.

'The Arnoteanus',' he said, 'the true-blood Arnoteanus...'

It was not the first time Pirgu had insisted to take us there. So, to shake him off, we promised to follow him wherever, whenever, but not that night. We parted near Mogoşoaia Bridge: Pirgu headed for the post office, while we broke off to Sărindar. The night was wet and chilly, and the fog was growing thicker. As my thoughts were slipping to the coziness of my sweet home bed, Pantazi, in his good old mood, beseeched my company for a while. This was something I couldn't dodge. Indeed, for his sake I could have jumped for the moon. For if my mind went freely with Paşadia, my heart went with Pantazi—and, whatever you might say, it's the heart that crowns the head, eventually. I had taken a fancy to this quaint character even before I met him: I felt I had found an age-old, long-lost friend, if not an alter-ego.

The Three Pilgrimages

C'est une belle chose, mon ami, que les voyages...[19]

Diderot[20]

A friend since time began—that was how I felt about him, although I had never met, or known anything about his way in the world until that blessed year, 1910. He showed up in Bucharest with the first sprouting leaves, and I often crossed his path as of that time.

What a sight for my eyes he was from the first time we met, and soon I would chase the next chance to see him again. Such characters do exist who, for no obvious reason, will awake our slumbering curiosity and stir our imagination to the point of weaving a tale around them. More than once have I admonished myself about my sensitivity to figures of this kind. After all, the misadventure with Sir Aubrey de Vere should have been enough warning—and yet, this time some new, overwhelming feeling was spurring my natural curiosity.

---

19 Voyages, my friend are a most gratifying pursuit...

20 Denis Diderot, an 18th century French philosopher, writer, art critic, was a prominent figure of the Enlightenment.

Could it be the fascination aroused by the man's melancholy appearance? Quite possible—in fact, if you only looked at his eyes you could read a world of meaning there. Half-hidden under deep brows, of a rare shade of blue, they gave off such a gentle, nostalgic gaze as seemed to be following in the footsteps of some olden dream.

Somehow, those same eyes would spell youthful vigour about this rather eccentric character, none of whose other features betrayed his age, in fact. They carried a serene radiance to his smooth forehead, complementing the marble-like pallor of his drawn, lean face in an aura of nobility. The tip of his chin hid under a goatee, soft as maize silk and of much the same colour. It was, in fact, the colour he usually chose for his suits. With him, everything carried the same soft, gentle, supple quality: his wear, his manners, his speech. Weary? Shy? Lordly? You might say he could be any or all of these. A dedicated loner, always trying to efface his presence in the crowd, he seemed to be surreptitiously sneaking along life's path. And yet, his intently modest appearance had the very opposite effect, as the more he tried to sink in the crowd, the more visible he came out, all the more out of place.

To be sure, a foreigner he was not, little resemblance though he bore to the stock native of this country, for his Romanian was so polished and refined, as was his French for that matter—only a shade less fluent, maybe. I had often enjoyed his casual company at the table, either in some classy bistro or on the porch of some cheap tavern. But the place where his essential melancholy mood came in deep resonance with my own frame of mind, to the point that I felt he mirrored my ego, was Cişmegiu[21]—the Cişmegiu of the good old days, a lonely, unkempt piece of land.

There, at dusk, this stranger used to promenade his wistful thoughts beneath the haughty crowns of tall trees. He paced intently, leaning on his cherry wood cane as he saun-tered along the alleys, smoking, and at times stopped still to rest on some stray thought. But what kind of thoughts were those, so piercing as to bring tears in his eyes?

The stars were in full bloom above his head when the dreamer would finally decide to leave for supper. Later, to-ward midnight, he turned up again at some drinking place where he usually stayed until closing time. Then he would leisurely walk the streets to meet the early morning light.

Like I said, I met the man all over the place. So famil-iar had I grown with his passing figure that I felt the day was unfulfilled when I hadn't seen him. Once I saw him at the railway station, he was taking the train to Arad[22], and I cringed with childish anguish at the thought I might lose my secret friend forever—the man whose gentle gaze would sweep the sky, the trees, the flowers, the children…

I knew his memory would have a tight grip on my mind, the more as he was, for me, an inherent detail of the larger picture of Cişmegiu, to which I had stayed in faith

---

21 Known today as Cişmigiu Gardens, the largest park in the central area of Bucharest, surrounding an artificial lake. Originally built in 1847, it has been redesigned several times along the years.

22 A city in western Transylvania.

even under the heavy rainfalls that came before the comet[23] that summer. The greenery of the garden, bursting with life under the prodigal showers, was a sight of lavish beauty in late afternoon, when the skies would clear in short respite. And then I lived the most gratifying evening when, on the big bridge across the lake, my heart thumped with joy at the sight of my friend.

Leaning against the frail, dilapidated balustrade, he was staring at the ivory glimmer of the rising Evening Star. He saw me smoking and asked for a light, and that was the beginning of the great thaw. I learnt I was no stranger to him either, since we had crossed each-other's path so often. He had been waiting for the right time to make my acquaintance, and he was grateful to the whim of hazard that made it happen that night.

'In the face of Beauty,' he explained, 'loneliness becomes oppressive; and this is indeed a beautiful night, my dear sir, worthy of blissful dreams and fairy tales. Now and then nights like this keep coming back, they say; and long ago, old masters would dip their pen in the subtle mystery of such nights to weave some sacred legend. But rarely did even the most consummate succeed to expose the true feeling of their deep-blue transparency. Such was the night when Hagar[24] was banned in the wilderness of Egypt. Bound by a magic spell, it seems, Time itself slows down its pace on an

---

23 Comet Halley was visible in 1910, which gives a further hint as to the time frame of the story.

24 See the Old Testament, Gen. 16:1-16; 21:8-21.

evening like this: no breath in the air, no rustle in the leaves, no ripple on the water…'

After all these years his voice is still ringing in my mind. His speech was slow and intent, even the humblest of words wrapped in the generous modulations of his warm deep voice. Under the veil of that all but mystical night, the intense blue of which swam in his eyes, in the overwhelming peace that resonated with his presence, I followed in his step, absorbing his elocution with insatiate gusto, all the way into the morning light. But as a one-night pocket was far from containing the huge baggage of his reflected experience, we parted upon an arranged appointment for the following evening. And this went on evening after evening, for the next three months, which I treasure as a rare treat in the course of my life. And the more the day shrank, the earlier we used to meet, and the later we parted. Had our company depended on the night's umbrella alone, I would never have missed the daylight: eternity beside him was such a joyous prospect with me. And yet, our pastime could be the very definition of monotony: our conversation would linger over supper until close to midnight, then we progressed as congenial peripatetic strollers often getting lost along slum lanes we had never known, so far as we even forgot we were in Bucharest. At times, when we came to an open spot, my man would stop to gaze at the sky, whose grace grew with the autumn season, and with every star of which he was quite familiar. In bad weather, we would go to his place.

He lived in Modei[25], a quiet street, on the second floor of a building belonging to King Carol, where an old Frenchwoman had let him two rooms furnished in the heavy taste of fifty years ago: a salon at the front and a bedroom at the back, separated by a tall glass partition. The tenant's obsessive fondness for flowers contributed a profusion of roses and tuberoses to the massive load of ebony and mahogany, silk, velvet, and mirrors—beautiful, frameless mirrors covering an entire wall. Complete with two silver chandeliers, each with five branches, all holding lively burning candles whenever we chanced to come by, the place bore the mark of refined sumptuousness which granted my host the perfect frame, in concord so close that, every time his figure comes to my mind, the setting follows suit...

But now the magic was setting in, for my man had begun to speak...

And the tale went on at a graceful pace, rich with the noblest fruit picked from the literary orchards of all peoples. A true master painter in words, he always found the best nuances to describe, albeit in a language he had long been estranged from, even the most sensitive and obscure attributes of nature, times or spaces, always to foster a perfect illusion. As if under a spell he carried my imagination along many a distant journey, the like of which I had never even dreamed

25 In the original: strada Modei (Fashion Street).

of. The man spoke on, and the yarn he spun wove a tapestry of enthralling fantasies at the back of my eyes.

Tall ruins robed in ivy folds sentinelled on the heights, and derelict city walls sagged under the weight of smothering verdure; deserted palaces lying in slumber in desolate gardens where some moss-clad stone idol cast an ethereal smile at the piles of rusty leaves being swept astray by the autumn wind; founts bereft of the last glimmering drop of water. Silvery threads of moonlight fondled old settlements sunken in blissful sleep, and sprightly flames glowed above the marshes. The clay and dirt that paved a thriving metropolis reflected the lights against the looming fog which thus became a chimerical blaze. But we would readily turn our back on the soot and slime of so defiled a place and flew away to meet the dizzy heights peaked with snow that bled in the sunset; we would leave behind flowery glades to clamber up in the cool shade of fir woods, lured by the rustle of creeks slithering their way down under the cover of thick fern. And so up we struggled, intoxicated by the crisp air, higher and higher we went. Down below, among barren slopes or hills crowned by leafy forests, green valleys cradled the winding rivers as they flowed away to melt in the distant haze that lingered above lush fields. A delicate murmur like a deep litany lined the pristine peace of that supreme wilderness while we watched the proud eagles hovering in the high skies over the deep of dark ravines. And the nights up there brought the stars so much closer. But there came the snow storms and the frost pushing us down south, toward realms whose names are music to the ear, where autumn lingers on till springtime and where everything, even pain and death, is received in a spirit of grace. Here, oleanders spread the bittersweet scent of their flowers across melancholy lakes that mirrored tall white towers among funereal cypresses. Like dedicated pilgrims, we went to pay reverence to Beauty in antique cities sunken in silence and oblivion, wandering their slant alleyways and squares invaded by green overgrowth. In ancient palaces and churches we stood in admiration of venerable masterpieces, sublime vestiges of the Past that breathed on us their magic-laden tale. The galley glided lazily between Hellenic and Roman shores. The last worn pillars of a pagan temple in ruin rose from amid a laurel grove. A Greek woman gave us a smile from a jasmine-curtained porch. We haggled with Armenian and Jewish merchants in bazaars, then joined the sailors for a jug of sweet wine in brothels, with belly dancers doing what they knew best. We were dazed contemplating the motley crowds swarming about the sunbathed markets, or the gentle sway of ship masts; we were entranced by the soothing silence of Turkish graveyards; we were elated at the distant sight of lavish white Oriental cities sprawled like idle odalisques in the shade of lofty cedars. Then we abandoned ourselves to the blue magic of the Mediterranean, the scorching heat of the enamelled skies, and the smothering dry winds of Lybia, till we finally sailed out into the ocean. To the northern skyline, the playful marriage of light and vapour was a blissful delight to the eye. The low mist left behind by the autumn drizzle bled in all colours of the rainbow under the spears of slanted sunrays, as did the hoar frost on leaves and petals. There was a volatile display of colours to seduce the eye—from heavy purple at sunset to violet blue to hoary transparencies in the long summer evenings, to the boreal magic above everlasting ice fields. We then turned to the tropics to share the farmers' tender dream of Florida and the Antilles; we sank into the murky selvas of the Amazon, with brightly coloured parrots flying past, to follow in the steps of "orchid hunters". Nothing escaped our greedy inquisitiveness: we sailed long voyages to discover spots of paradise lost in the middle of the peaceful ocean, then headed for the lands of spices, cradle of ancient civilisations, to celebrate the coming of spring at Ise[26], then abandoned ourselves to the mystic magic of Chinese and Indian nights, or to the thrill of evenings at the waterfront in Bangkok, with the hot breeze gently stroking the silver bells of pagodas or the large leaves of tropical trees. Europe was far behind, and all we had cherished about it was by now a dim, fading memory. And on we went, in quest of ever deeper horizons, older forests, loftier ruins, gardens with more than an abundant profusion of flowers. Contentment was briefly reached at the far end of exotic beauty or variance, when the dream became nearly as tangent to our senses as real life. But however great the wonder, either at the flighty play of nature or some breathtaking vestige bearing the mark of human genius, it would not last—and on we journeyed, across bleak stretches and rugged wilderness; we avoided the desolation of the barren desert or the ghostly fetid swamps, eager to set foot on the sea shore again.

O yes, the sea...

---

26 Ise is a temple of the Japanese goddess Amaterasu, incarnation of the Sun in Shinto religion.

Smooth and glossy like a shallow pool, and fencing within her winding coastline the perfect reflection of the turquoise blue of the vault of heaven and the ivory clouds; now an affluence of colours like a mad flowery meadow at the height of spring, then a fireworks of sparks like a vast swarm of fireflies; now faded and flat, then alive and restless, bustling and foaming toward the heaven whose daughter she is. Of her he spoke in pagan adoration, suffice it to mention her name and his voice quivered in subdued undertones, as if he were confessing to some deep secret or murmuring a prayer. Words, he thought, were less than could aptly praise the sea, her vast rolling power, the unfettered pristine womb of teeming life. He thought even the most acclaimed of poets had failed in their venture to celebrate her majesty. Forever did the sea whisper at the back of his mind, forever did her roar ring against the walls of his heart, as if forever locked in a loving shell; and in her bosom, the ultimate passion of his lifetime, did he wish to rest his bones at the end of his earthly passage...

...he fell silent, gazing ahead. For some time I had been feeling a heavy pressure against my chest and temples. Oddly enough, this man, who cherished the sharp winds of the open sea and the salubrious smell of algae, abhorred open windows and lived in a close room with stagnant air packed with smoke and stale odours. As the hours passed, the candle flames stood still and, at times, I heard a shy rustle as another dead petal dropped from the withered roses.

That was not the only quirk he had. Sometimes, he reminded me of that young Englishman whose sad story I once recounted: he had much the same way of richly adorning his travelogues with rare historical details; he, too, had inquired each and every place he had visited, land or water, about what lay in its history, and had blended today's view into yesterday's vision. He had stood in daydream at the foot of the cliff that had seen Sapho[27] plunge into the waves, or on the shore where Pompey[28] had been burnt on a pyre. Here, the beautiful Ines[29] was murdered; and there, the demented king died in confinement. But while the vast panoramas so masterfully described by Sir Aubrey were void of all living human presence, as if in the aftermath of a deluge, those of my new friend were teeming with a motley crowd, their attire a dazzling fantasy of colours: sheiks and pashas, emirs and khans, rajahs and mandarins, clergy and friars of all faiths and orders, fortune tellers, hermits, sorcerers, healers, chieftains of nomadic tribes whose guest he had been or with whom he had feasted or hunted, and he must have humoured them as he had his many friends back in Europe, presenting them with his affable, convivial character, lenient and free of all vulgar pride or prejudice, which proved him a sterling

---

27 A 7th-6th century B.C. Greek poetess who killed herself plunging off a tall cliff into the sea on Leuce island.

28 Pompey, Cneius (106 □48 B.C.), surnamed the Great, Roman general and statesman. At a point of his career, he entered into rivalry with Cæsar; after a desperate struggle he was defeated at Pharsalia, and escaping to Egypt, was assassinated there by orders of Ptolemy XII, in a boat close to the shore.

29 Inês Pérez de Castro, favourite lover of infante Don Pedro of Portugal, was assassinated in 1335 by order of King Alfons IV. When Pedro succeeded to the throne, he had her exhumed and declared her his wife, therefore Queen of Portugal.

gentleman, a late vestige of what the "old gentility" held the most in favour. And I was not so much curious about the background of this Mr. Pantazi, as I had heard he was called—this Beauty-addict person who had fed on all knowledge of the world, who would read Cervantes and Camões[30] in the original and converse in Romany with the beggars, this knight of St. George of Russia—, as I was perplexed by the mystifying melancholy of this spoiled child of fate, a kind of mild pensiveness enshrouding him in a romantic aura redolent of faraway skies, shores and seas. His evocation of such alluring places had fashioned my soul to a nomad's, agonising with wanderlust into the unknown, seduced by the prospect of boundless roaming. To think that I might forever be fettered to a patch of land in smothering frustration was excruciating torture. Like the magic spear which itself was the very cure to the wounds it had inflicted, my strange friend's stories were at once ravage and remedy; I drifted like drunk into a world of dream, as if I had smoked poppy or hemp, stirring my fantasy to boiling point, only to awake to bitter awareness.

And so, I had once more made friends with a stranger. We were quite close, most of the time; I was welcome in his house at any hour, day or night, to the point that I had come to spend more time at his place rather than mine. With autumn setting in he became more reluctant to go out; he was very sensitive to cold, and in bleak weather he would keep

---

30 Luís Vaz de Camões, the greatest poet of Portugal, whose poetic artistry was compared to that of Shakespeare.

the curtains drawn across the windows and the lights on all through the day. Then he got nostalgic about a certain villa waiting for him somewhere on a sea shore, under warm skies, in an abundance of green foliage and flowers. Flowers—oh, did he love flowers! The last roses had withered in his vases and as the chrysanthemums that replaced them gave off no scent, he had placed around large bowls with bundles of vanilla rolls in them. On small tables sweetmeats, fruits and refreshments were an open invitation to the guest. He lived a life of perfect aloofness, with no care whatsoever about anybody or anything. Lying reclined against soft cushions, he smoked incessantly while telling stories, and sometimes fell silent and sank in deep thought, tears trickling down his cheeks. And I didn't know of another guest he might have had besides me.

Now here we are, some four weeks before the evening that opened our story, in the same French bistro where Mr Pantazi enjoyed a permanent reservation in the most private corner. At supper time, a cacophonous crowd bustled in and started fretting about in the confined space of the tiny pub. I don't know what exactly had brought together the cream of Bucharest's back-alley world; but I remember that the moment I had just decided to turn my back on the vain, hollow sight and give full attention to the dish under my eyes, two characters entered the place, who were, if anything, hard to ignore. For a moment I had the feeling I was looking at two famished beasts slipping their way into the pen against the silly bustle of a herd of ignorant bull calves. It was one of those hand-in-glove combinations, welded tight by the daemon of depravity to the point that they eventually lose all sense of individuality. It must have been the case with these two, for what if not depravity could have stuck together such perfectly divergent figures? One was an elderly apparition, smartened up in a desperate renovation attempt, his hair dyed dark; his body, stiff though fairly supple still, was topped with a head such as you would hardly get a chance to contemplate in our times: a face written in lines of haughty grimness telling of ruthless, fiendish defiance. The other was much younger, yet worn and bloated, a pointed tummy pushing out above a pair of thin, bracketed legs; his thick-lipped face wore a slimy grin that spelt the basest of baseness. The former had swept an icy gloomy gaze above the heads in the room; the latter was squinting fidgety vicious glances about. The overall impression he gave off did him no credit whatsoever, and the company of the lofty gentleman only emphasised his impudent cast of a dedicated rotter.

'You wouldn't even find the water in a pool,' he grumbled, loud enough for us to hear. 'It's always got to be me, always Pirgu, poor soul!' He grasped Pantazi's hand in a familiar handshake, then mine in a patronising squeeze, and nonchalantly sat down at our table without deeming it necessary to ask permission. His companion, however, remained standing until the proper introductions were made—a ritual I enjoyed the more as I had long hoped for these two personages to meet. To my mind, Paşadia and Pantazi were twin souls destined to blend and value each-other.

We held the house open through the night. Pirgu left and returned several times, each time more inebriated than before. To assure Pantazi of his dedicated affection, he kept calling him "master" and smothered him with exuberant kisses.

'Stop me kissing him, brothers, before he's good for Govora[31]!'

Paşadia came to the rescue:

'Behave, you infamous clown, or we may as well send you to Mărcuţa[32]!'

In that case, you might say it was the right place for all of the other three of us, never to be let loose—because, for the sake of being together, Pantazi and I sailed in the wake of Paşadia's nightly course, who, in his turn, abandoned himself blindly to Pirgu's delirious guidance. I was thus introduced into a world the existence of which I had never suspected. Had somebody else told me there was such depravity and degradation in Bucharest as met my eyes, I would have dismissed it as a whim of their imagination. The city had remained steeped in an inveterate tradition of chronic decadence. With every step we were inevitably reminded we were at the gates of the Orient. To me, however, debauchery was less reason for perplexity than the sheer madness covering all ranks and stations. I must confess it was beyond my ultimate expectation to see such abundance of insanity at large, such perversion as would exceed the span of even the most morbid imagination. I met not a single soul but was possessed of some vicious flaw or, when I least expected, dropped some

31 Govora is a spa in Vâlcea county, southern Romania, known for the therapeutic properties of several mineral springs.

32 At the time, a sanatorium and mental asylum.

massive nonsense—which eventually drained me of all hope to meet sanity in the flesh. Of the very few cases still worthy of some interest, Paşadia was the only one I could eventually single out.

I have mentioned how my distinguished friend had, some fifteen years before, put an end to the long struggle his bitter fate had forced him into, only to bury himself alive. Since then, everything he did was so reckless and senseless that you couldn't help joining the wide suspicion as to his being mentally deranged. In his furious hatred of Romania, he had vowed to himself that, as soon as he could afford the slightest means, he would forever and completely estrange himself from this country. And yet, when wealth had favoured him at last, not only did he never again think of crossing the border, but, against the darkest of all possible anticipation, he chose Bucharest to settle down of all places, the very cradle of his most heartbreaking memories. He fully renovated Zinca Mamonoaia's old houses, a bargain he had picked up at an auction, stuffed them with all kinds of rare and valuable assets, and thus made them into his own secluded sanctuary to live a lavish, lordly life. However, eccentric was the least you could call his ways. A cook and a butler had been kept in his service for a full fifteen years, although he only dined evenings, and always at the bistro. For as long, he had never come home to sleep in his own bed. Like speechless ghosts, his servants shuffled in and away upon his call, but he could not otherwise bear their standing presence under his roof. Therefore, they were free to live a life of ease in a nearby lodge, where they had coupled and bred and brought their larger families and friends to stay, of whom the landlord had no acquaintance whatsoever. Word was spread that one day, as he was looking out of the window, he saw a coffin being carried out of his courtyard and didn't as much as care to know who the deceased was. A full account of his eccentricities would take forever, so I shall confine myself to the most amazing: Paşadia lived two alternate lives.

From morning till evening he would not budge from home, would not rise from among the books and papers spread across his desk: he kept reading and writing, without as much as lighting a cigarette all this time—he only took an occasional sip out of a cup of strong, black, sugarless coffee. I sometimes called to see him—and each such visit was a day to remember. What a noble character, indeed! What an unfathomable steep from his ethereal height to the turbid waters of the most below! Not a trace in him of the consecrated local profanity—nothing Balkanic, nothing gypsy-like. Walking his threshold was crossing the border into civilisation. It was a shelter for solemn spiritual relief. But then again, how could it be that a man of such accomplished culture and courtesy, who would have ranged with the cream of Weimar society, should plunge into regular night-long depravity in the wake of Pirgu's kind? How could the western aristocrat take pleasure in tasting the smoke-dried salt meat and the thick new wine, the beef-bowel soup and the marc brandy? How could a classic Viennese, imbued with Mozart's magic, lend his ear to the *ciamparale* and the *bidineaua*[33]? Was it that his will was somehow smothered along these spells? Or was he an innocent victim of some odd, transient affliction? I could hardly think otherwise, and I doubt there could be a better

---

33 Gypsy dances.

answer for anyone who had an idea of the gruesome ancestry Paşadia was doomed to drag behind.

It was nearly a century since the first man known to have borne this name, to which the surname of Măgureanu had been appended to confirm ownership of a small estate received as a token of voivodal generosity, had fled some remote Turkish province to avoid the dire consequences of double murder and come to settle in Wallachia, where he eventually got to be appointed provost marshal in the voivode's service. This ill-reputed immigrant with a history of bloodshed behind had never been seen to laugh, they said. As rumour had it, he never mentioned his parentage, presumably from shame of an undistinguished descent. On the other hand, the man betrayed, in both body and spirit, the regular features of a noble lineage in decay. His lofty conduct and noble appearance blended with a haughty, bitterly determined, hateful and cruel character and a penchant for idleness and taedium vitae. All these ingredients he passed on to his descendants who, had they not struggled among themselves, forever divided and contentious, could have built a powerful dynasty of excellence. They believed, and not without reason, that Wallachia was inauspicious to them, but the adversities piling up against them were no less kindled by their own passionate, rebellious, intractable disposition. Their voracious scholarly appetite had gained them distinguished eloquence in both speech and writing; however, despite their brilliance and resourcefulness, there was little trace of a distinct purpose to whatever pursuit they engaged in. Whimsical, extravagant and prankish, every one of them carried deep inside the seed of their own decline and demise. Hovering

over the destiny of the Paşadia-Măgureanu breed, one might
be tempted to detect a fatal pattern relentlessly driving the lot
to extinction, at the end of a massive flow of afflictions. Up-
rooted and transplanted into alien soil, the old stem had dole-
fully lost its last leaves to the savage blasts. The murderous
marshal had died an untimely death, supposedly poisoned by
his own kin. The other one, the cavalry commander, a glum
hunter who lived most of his life in Vlăsia[34], was charged
with highway robbery and forged coinage and disappeared,
never to be heard of again. His son, my friend's father, a
mean, fiendish parent, was an addicted gambler and drunkard
who, after having staked and lost several pieces of inherited
property, perished in the agony of mental dissolution. His
young cousin, the poet, met a similar fate; and of the girls,
the only one to have come under a bride's wreath died an
atrocious death as her hair caught fire from a candle on her
wedding night. The women who served to perpetuate the
breed—from the grumpy, headstrong Greek who would forever mutter and splutter in inveterate discontent among casks
full of oranges, to the wicked and scrawny Serb who had spit
the Holy Communion bread and wine into the priest's beard
and cursed her children with her last breath, to the mean and
sickly woman from Braşov[35], eaten alive with cancer and
hate—had infused their own poison to an already tainted
bloodline, only to swell a nefarious legacy of flaws and in-
firmity. Along with it, however, that seed of uncannily morbid intelligence was carried a few generations further, to
reach the peak of sterile brilliance in this last descendant. In

---

34 A heavily forested area in southern Romania.

35 A city in the central part of Romania.

him the ghosts of his progenitors nested in muffled spite which sparked in his glum eye or sneered in his baleful grin. They had hampered his progress and nullified all chance of a glorious retirement; they had ruined the balance of his brilliant talents, plunging him into bitter and often exhaustive resistance and self-struggle, far more consuming than the confrontations with his living enemies. It was in this visceral assault that he lost the more battles, till one day he took the grim decision to let the daemons have their share and allowed himself to sink in depravity. But then, I feel it my duty to say it again: not for a moment did depravity come to taint his dignity—for if the patrician would, under night's brow, step down into Suburra[36], he gave up none of his aristocratic attire or any other marks of distinction. He remained the same stately figure in vice as in virtue. His individuality was then possessed of an uncanny metamorphosis as he followed limp in Pirgu's wake, a golem whose eyes shone with a feeble glint of dejection reflecting the most devastating despondency. He could be sitting there on countless cigarettes and wine glasses, perfectly speechless, till the night gave in. Fortunately, I knew the way to call him back—and there the man came suddenly alive, his hazy eyes lighting up and a melancholy smile sprouting shyly on his weary face. I had brought word about olden times. I knew that if there was anything to bring him back to life, it was a vision of times of yore: he would embrace the subject with almost religious, mystical fervour while indulging in the superstitious belief that his ripened, hardened soul had wandered the world in many a bodily frame before. In fact, it was the only fantasy he com-

---

36 A lower-class, ill-famed district of ancient Rome.

plied to entertain, in mild consolation for a bitter life. So compelling was that vision in him that he couldn't help sharing it directly with Pantazi and me; and the magic struck again as we were led to journey with him across the glorious realms of olden days. The age that lured us the most with a nostalgic draw was that of the eighteenth century.

All three of us were the would-be offspring of grand dynasts, all three Knights Hospitallers of the Order of St John of Jerusalem, also known as Knights of Malta, proud to wear the white enamelled cross-and-crown trophy hanging to a flaxen black ribbon on our chests. We had come into the world in the late years of the Sun King, been raised by Jesuite monks, and Villena[37] had initiated us in the profession of arms. We were quite young when, sailing with a convoy, we sank several barbarian vessels; later on we championed in the field for the glory of the Lilies[38]: we served under Berwick[39] at Kehl, and under Coigny[40] at Gustalla, after which exploits

37 A town in the province of Valencia, Spain.

38 In heraldry, lilies spelt royalty. France was also known as the Kingdom of Lilies (Le royaume des lys). In the 17th century, the Knights of Malta added four lilies to the four arms of the eight-point Maltese Cross.

39 Jacques de Berwick (1670-1734), a French general and natural son of King James II of England, led the French army in the Rhine battles against the Germans, at Kehl and Philippsburg. He died in the Philippsburg battle.

40 Franquetot de Coigny (1670-1759), French marshal, defeated the German army at Guastalla in 1734.

we hung up our swords and, eager to discover the most of what there was, the three of us went to follow in the tracks of Peterborough[41]. Courtiers of noble blood, there was no single Court across Europe we left unattended; their stairs resounded with our red-heeled steps, their mirrors reflected our haughty countenances and inscrutable smiles; we visited Court after Court through the round, welcomed and honoured in every place, distinguished guests of all Highnesses, Graces and Holinesses, of Princes high and low, of Abbesses and Fathers Superior and Bishops; we were blessed with a life of ease and comfort at Belem and Granja, at Favorita and Caserta, at Versailles, Chantilly and Sceaux, at Windsor, Amalienborg, Nymphenburg and Herrenhausen, at Schonbrunn and Sans-Souci, at Haga-on-the-Maelar, at the Hermitage and at Peterhof[42]. Through day and night we rolled on a feasting

---

41 Charles Mordaunt, 3rd Earl of Peterborough and 1st Earl of Monmouth (1658-1735), English general and politician.

42 Boroughs and residential seats of European royalty. At Belem, near Lisbon, there is a monastery hosting the tombs of Portuguese kings; in Granja stands the summer palace of Spanish kings, built by Philip V near Segovia; Favorita: a name given to several entertainment palaces like Mantua in Italy, Rastatt in Baden, or Vienna (apparently the Ludwigsburg castle of the Wurttemberg dynasty); Caserta: a town in southern Italy, with a summer palace of the kings of Naples and the two Sicilies; Versailles: the famous residence and sumptuous gardens of French kings, outside Paris; Chantilly: a town near Paris, mostly known for the reputable medieval castle renovated by Louis XIV; Sceaux: a town 10 kms south of Paris with a castle built by architect Colbert and which hosted a literary club; Windsor: the castle built by Edward III by the Thames, one of the British royal residences into our days; Amalienburg: the royal palace in Copenhagen; Nymphenburg: a castle and park of Bavarian royalty, in the north-west of Munich; Herrenhausen: the Guelfs' castle near Hanover, complete with a park and an open-air theatre; Schönbrunn: the Austrian emperors' summer

spree like never before and never after, regaling on the most gratifying delights of body and mind along the most prodigal of all centuries, the epitome of lavishness, lust and lustre, to be equalled only by its lack of glory—in short, the age swept and spurred by the French spirit, when Cupids took the place of Cherubs even in churches and hearts were longing with passion, hopelessly subdued by the blindfolded god. And so we were there to see the Well-Beloved crawling at the feet of the marquise[43], the Potsdam Philosopher[44] whimpering for Kayserlinck, and Moscow's Semiramis[45] broken-hearted at Lanskoy's decease. Indeed, we ourselves did not escape the luscious corrupting spell (*the nightfall, so lovely under the tall chestnut trees...*[46]). But following the perverse mood of political teachings, we made of the ladies a treasure as much as a measure of our pursuits, as through silk-lined boudoirs

residence, with a vast Versailles-style park; Sans-Souci: Frederick the Great's favourite residence near Potsdam, later a summer palace for Prussian kings; Hague on the Maelar: a city in Holland with a sumptuous royal palace built in 1644; Hermitage: a palace built by Russian empress Catherine II in Petersburg, today an art museum; Peterhof: a township founded by Peter the Great in 1711 by Kronstadt Bay, with an imposing palace.

43 Reference is made to King Louis XV (1710-1774), also called le Bien-Aimé, and to Antoinette Poisson (1721-1764), Marquise de Pompadour, who greatly influenced him.

44 King Frederick II the Great of Prussia (1712-1786), author of Anti-Machiavel and other studies, also referred to as 'the Potsdam philosopher', or 'the Sans-Souci philosopher'.

45 Catherine II of Russia (1729-1796), also called the Semiramis of the North.

46 Possibly an intended paraphrase of a cue from Beaumarchais' play Le mariage de Figaro (IV, 3): "Qu'il fera beau, ce soir, sous les grands marroniers".

we made our way to the company and service of the Chosen and the Mighty.

Lurking in the shadows, we were no strangers to every intrigue and conspiracy, and nothing was foiled or favoured without our agency: flattery and courtesy would buy royal confidants, courtesans or beaus; high officials were advised and guided by us while we abstrusely arranged for their rise or fall depending on circumstances. We were then engaged in sundry commissions: escort Belle-Isle[47] to Frankfurt to arrange for the election of the emperor; set out on a matchmaking expedition to Dresden with Richelieu[48]; negotiate paintings by Watteau[49] in Paris for Frederick the Great; carry Elisabeth Petrovna's[50] rough diamonds to Amsterdam to be polished; order fine lace in Malines for Brühl[51]. Goaded by some restless imp of adventure, we did all that in candid disdain for wealth or honours, only to stay on the move. In-

---

47 Charles Louis Auguste Fouquet de Belle Isle (1684-1761), Superintendent of Finances under King Louis XV of France; in 1741 he was sent to Germany as French plenipotentiary to carry out, in the interests of France, a grand scheme of political reorganization of the empire and to obtain the election of Charles, Elector of Bavaria as emperor.

48 Armand de Richelieu (1696-1788), marshal of France, notorious for his frivolous life, great-grandson to Cardinal Richelieu.

49 Antoine Watteau (1684-1721), French painter of the Rococo period.

50 Elisabeth Petrovna (1709-1762), empress of Russia, daughter to Peter the Great and Catherine I.

51 Heinrich von Brühl (1700-1763), famous German politician, noted for his intrigues and a penchant for luxury.

curable vagrants, forever on the road, hopelessly inquisitive and never tired to taste the pleasures of life, we frantically spent our breath riding along the most exuberant age ever known to history, sharing in its bounty and madness to our hearts' desire.

We followed the mainstream spirit of music: we stood up for Rameau[52] and Glück[53], and, just like the three Magi, went to pay homage to the infant who was to grow into the figure of Mozart[54]. We followed the mainstream spirit of adventure: Neuhof[55], Bonneval[56], Cantacuzen[57], Tarakhanova[58],

---

52 Jean-Philippe Rameau (1683-1764), French composer and music theorist, author of a revolutionary Treatise on Harmony (1722) which ruffled the tradition and caused him fierce attacks by supporters of the Italian opera.

53 Christoph Willibald Glück (1714-1784), German composer and innovator in opera.

54 Wolfgang Amadeus Mozart (1756-1791), celebrated German pianist and composer; when he was only 7, his father Leopold Mozart accompanied him on a concert tour to West Germany, Holland, Paris and London.

55 Theodor von Neuhof (1686-1756), an adventurist who made his way to the throne of Corsica in 1736, under the name of Theodore I, only to be banished by Genoese and French troops two years later.

56 Claude-Alexandre de Bonneval (1675-1747), French general who lived an adventurous life, serving in turn France, Austria, and finally Turkey, where Sultan Ahmed III made him a pasha.

57 Cantacuzen (phonetic adaptation of Cantacuzéne, the French spelling of Cantacuzino), a famous noble family whose Byzantine branch fled west after the fall of Constantinople, and whose descendants there became merchants, scholars, or adventurers. Wallachian voivodes Şerban and Ştefan, and Moldavian voivode Dimitrie were offsprings of yet another branch

the Duchess of Kingston[59], the Knight of Eon[60], Zanovich[61], Trenck[62]— all of them enjoyed our service, either secretly or

---

of the same Cantacuzino family tree. The frequent references to empress Catherine II in this chapter may hint to Mihail Cantacuzino, former ban (a provincial governor) of Craiova, who left the country for Russia in 1776, where the empress conferred on him the rank of General and where he compiled a genealogy of the Cantacuzino family in 1787.

58 Isabella Tarakhanova (1755-1777), illegitimate daughter to Tsarina Elisabeth Petrovna and feldmarshal Razumovsky, claimed the throne of Poland. Upon request of Catherine II, she was arrested in Italy. She manages to escape and, with the help of Prince Stanislaw Radziwill (1734-1790), prepares to go to Poland. She is conjured to come to St Petersburg by Count Alexander Orloff (the assassin of Tsar Peter III) and drowns in prison during the 1777 floodings.

59 Elisabeth Chudleigh, Duchess of Kingston (1720-1788), a notorious adventurer; wife to Lord Bristol, then to the Duke of Kingston, mistress of King George II, then of King Frederick the Great of Prussia; she was tried and condemned for bigamy.

60 Charles de Beaumont d'Eon (1728-1810), a French adventurer and spy, political and diplomatic agent with several European royal courts. At St. Petersburg he is said to have disguised as a woman and served Empress Elisabeth as a "lecture companion". His gender was a matter of hot debate at the time, till upon his death he was discovered to be anatomically male.

61 Ştefan Zanovici, or Zanowitch (1751-1785), an adventurer of Albanian descent; he tried to substitute himself for Tsar Peter III; in Poland, he called himself Castrioto de Albania; in the war between Austria and the Netherlands he appeared under the name of Stepan Hannibal and traded with the States General (the parliament of the Netherlands) an imaginary Montenegran army for 80,000 florins; soon discovered in Habsburg, he was arrested and killed himself by cutting his veins.

openly; we helped a debilitated and decrepit Casanova to find refuge with Waldstein at Dux[63]. We were no less attracted to the uncanny and the supernatural: barren of all commonsensical belief, we chose to give credit to such eccentric contrivances as the mirror of Saint Germain[64], Cagliostro's[65] carafe, Mesmer's[66] tub, or Swedenborg's[67] and Schrepfner's[68] oddi-

---

62 Friedrich von der Trenck (1726-1794), an officer under Frederick the Great, was arrested and detained for a long time on grounds of a romantic affair with the king's sister Amelie. He later turns up in Paris and ends up on the scaffold as a foreign power agent.

63 Giacomo Girolamo Casanova de Seingalt (1725-1798) was a Venetian adventurer and notorious womanizer, to the point as his name has become an emblem of the art of seduction. He was, by vocation and avocation, a lawyer, clergyman, military officer, violinist, con man, pimp, businessman, diplomat, spy, politician, mathematician, social philosopher, cabalist, playwright, and writer. He associated with European royalty and clergy, along with such luminaries as Voltaire, Goethe and Mozart. Casanova spent his last years in Bohemia as a librarian in Count Waldstein's household, where he also wrote the story of his life, Histoire de ma vie, which is referred to as a reliable source describing the social customs and norms of 18th century Europe.

64 The Count of Saint-Germain (1710-1780), a controversial figure described as a courtier, adventurer, charlatan, inventor, alchemist, pianist, violinist and amateur composer. All but a legend, St. Germain is often connected with stories of occultism and theosophy, and was claimed to have incredible magical powers.

65 Count Alessandro di Cagliostro (1743-1795) was the alias of the occultist Giuseppe Balsamo, an Italian adventurer who staged and conducted spiritualist sessions in most great European cities. Implicated in the Diamond Necklace Affair (1785), which compromised Queen Maria Antoinette herself, Balsamo ended up with a death sentence which Pope Pius VI switched to life imprisonment in 1791.

66 Franz Anton Mesmer (1734-1815), a physicist, issued the theory on animal magnetism. Mesmerism advocated inducing a 'magnetic sleep' (hypnotism) as a cure for various afflictions. A wooden tub was an auxiliary device he used during his treatment sessions. Dr.

ties. On the other hand, we also followed closely the exploits of Scheele[69] or Lavoisier[70]. We had befriended most of those whose names history could not possibly ignore; we exchanged epistles, we often took a turn to Montbard[71] or Ferney[72], made delightful long stops to visit Hoditz[73] in his Silesian Arcadia of Rosswalde; we would add up to the em-

---

Mesmer issued his conclusions in Memoire sur la découverte du Magnétisme Animal in 1779.

67 Emmanuel von Swedenborg (1688-1772), Swedish naturalist and mystic. Following a 'mystical vision' he claimed to have had in London in 1734, he founded a new religion whose terms he exposed in his theosophical work Vera christiana religio.

68 Johann Georg Schrepfner (or Schrepfer) (1730-1774), a German adventurer and charlatan who founded a secret association of purported masonic orientation.

69 Karl Wilhelm Scheele (1742-1786), Swedish chemist, discoverer of oxygen, hydrogen, chlorine and manganese; he also discovered the arsenic, oxalic, tartaric and prussic acids.

70 Antoine Lavoisier (1743-1794), one of the founders of modern chemistry, the first to demonstrate the importance of oxygen in burning processes.

71 Montbard, a town by the Burgogne Canal in France, known for the nearby castle which was the residence of the famed naturalist Buffon (1707-1788).

72 Ferney, a town in the Ain district, where Voltaire lived and worked between 1758 and 1788.

73 Albert Joseph von Hoditz (1706-1778), Prussian earl, army general and friend of Frederick the Great's. Von Hoditz would stage theatrical and pastoral performances at his Rosswalde estate. Mateiu I. Caragiale planned to write a Hoditz monograph (as apparent in his notes in 1935), but he died before he could accomplish it.

press' suite in Tauris[74], or dissipate in the sheer madness of the Venice carnival; and, behind yet another display of masks, it was in our arms that the king succumbed when shot by Ankarstroem in Venice's northern sister-city[75]. The stars had decided that the most glamorous of all centuries should end in bloodshed—and when, a few months later, seeing the head of Madame de Lamballe[76] stuck on a spike amidst a sea of cocky Phrygian caps[77], we understood that our time had passed and all we had so dearly cherished would soon fall prey to destruction and chaos, we covered our faces and vanished forever.

'Time you dropped all this balderdash, gents, and got to something serious—like skirts, for instance.' This was Pirgu, sour and surly with our, to him, esoteric excursion.

---

74 A Russian guberniya (province) in the Crimean Peninsula, with Simferopol as its capital city. The ancient Greeks called Crimea Tauris (later Taurica), after its inhabitants, the Tauri.

75 On March 16, 1792, King Gustav III of Sweden was fatally wounded by Ankarstroem (Anckarström) who shot him during a fancy dress ball at the Royal Opera House in Stockholm and died two weeks later.

76 Marie Thérèse-Louise, Princess of Lamballe (1749-1792), maid of honour and private companion of Marie Antoinette's, was sentenced and executed by the French Revolution's tribunal in September 1792.

77 The Phrygian cap, named named after Phrygia (formerly a kingdom in Anatolia, nowadays Turkey), was adopted in ancient Greece and Rome, and later by several European cultures. During the French Revolution it became an emblem of liberty and freedom.

At that point I knew the ground was getting hot, for Paşadia denied Pirgu all competence or taste regarding the fair sex while the latter claimed, with no less conviction, that Paşadia was a duffer when it came to ladies. Now, judging by the kind of women Pirgu used to submit to Paşadia, anyone would have embraced the latter's opinion—for they were all the scum and dregs of the gender, each and every one of them. But then the frowning question came: why would someone like Paşadia, whose money could easily buy the crème de la crème, so loosely indulge such gross humiliation from Gorică, whose brute instincts did not, after all, exclude a certain taste in women. Gorică Pirgu definitely had an experience of combing the slums for fair maidens whom he would then lure with the vision of a comfortable, wealthy life and, like a true father, protectively tend their early steps along the road of vice, never touching them himself in an unbecoming way. Far from whatever smelt like pure, unadulterated flesh, his senses were directed on a very different path, to be only aroused by the fumes of alcohol—and then he needed the ravaged, crippled kind, toothless, hunchbacked or pregnant, oversized specimens of the fair sex, behemoths to crush the scales at St. George's[78]. Hogs and apes would have turned their heads if they had heard and understood the stories he was so proud to tell about what he did with the poor things.

'Don't spit on it, or you'll spoil the flavour,' he sneered. 'I can't help it, what!—it's my own fancies riding me down!'

---

78 An old church in downtown Bucharest, outside which petty peddlers would let you read your weight for small change.

The storm had barely died down when it was followed by an encore, out of the blue—for Paşadia would never waste a chance to spit his venom on everything Romanian. In moderation, Pantazi was always on his side. With one of them it came from the rage against a loved one who had betrayed him, while the other was just mildly contemptuous of a poor relative. At the very opposite, Pirgu's patriotic fancies could be a matter of amazement to his own self. I will not forget the day when I went to call for him at a snobbish gathering of upstarts, all dressed up in national costumes, while none actually speaking a word of Romanian; I was dumbfounded to see him there, a candid shepherd of the Carpathians in sweet effigy, frantically whirling round in a folk dance with Papura Jilava, a dedicated theosophist. Overly sensitive when it came to hearing his poor dear country being snubbed and scoffed at, he would abruptly stand up and leave us. Not for long though, for he would turn up shortly and never alone, always to deliver his collected fauna at our table without as much as asking permission. This is how I came to contemplate, in less than a month's time, a parade of the most decadent, decrepit, delirious, disgraced figures of Bucharest human stock. Lost in his usual reverie, Pantazi hardly noticed them. As for Paşadia, it was amazing to see his grumpiness yield to a perfectly civil and affable conduct while wining and dining them, shaking hands with them and asking them a few well-chosen questions that gave away a certain knowledge of the world which contradicted his apparent aloofness. However, he grew red with resentment whenever Pirgu arrived with Poponel[79], arm in arm, hollering a dirty army song.

The character known by this alias was a civil servant of the Ministry of Foreign Affairs, a very promising young fellow who had, like many in his line of business, a peculiar taste for a certain unorthodox approach under hot dispute. Indeed, he had proved himself quite worthy of such spiritual patrons as Lamsdorf[80], Eulenburg[81], or Mestschersky. Since there were not many dedicated içoğlans[82] in town at that time, Poponel was looked upon as a rare bird. Far from what you could commonly deem attractive, his frame and figure harboured a woman's soul, scorched and consumed by the fire of Sodom, the soul of a sleazy harlot idling about the soldier barracks at nightfall. I shall spare the page further description of him, for I would have to dip my pen in nothing less than slimy filth and rotting pus—and even so, not only

---

79 In Romanian, a humorous nickname for a homosexual.

80 Vladimir Lamsdorf (1841-1907), a Russian statesman of German descent who served as Foreign Minister between 1900 and 1906. His political authority was shaken by speculations about his sexual orientation.

81 Philipp von Eulenburg (1847-1921), a German politician and diplomat in the late 19th-early 20th century. Although married, Eulenburg reportedly had homosexual affairs with members of the Kaiser's inner circle and was publicly exposed in 1907.

82 In Turkish it means a footboy, or a page, to serve a sultan. The term was adopted in Romanian with the same meaning, in relation to some of the country's rulers. In this context, the word is a slang metaphor for 'pederast'.

the pen would be defiled, but it would be an insult to the filth and the pus. But hardly was he to blame at all—after all, it was the stuff he had been born of. And when this diplomat showed up, Pașadia would sink back into his sombre slumber until he left; then he would rise to lash out at Pirgu with bitter reproof. And Pirgu stood up to the charge.

'When are you ever going to give up all this flat prejudice?' he said. 'Why all this vicious persecution? Or maybe you'd rather he proposed to you? No? You wouldn't? Then what's biting you against him? Aren't you hiring your own Russkii hackney coachman by the month? So why'n't you let him hire his own Turkish stallion by the month? Anyone mind the tarts and sluts you go for in your fishpond? They don't, do they? So why on earth would you pick on the young male fish in his pond?'

'All right,' Pașadia insisted, 'but then why does he keep nursing them like that?'

'Well, you see,' Pirgu explained, 'if he didn't, they wouldn't suckle him, would they?'

An accomplished devil's disciple indeed! Had he ever contemplated committing to paper the paradox of his scholarly ignorance and lack of any and all ideal combined with his consummate art of gross derision and his sagacious knowledge of that underworld of hoodlums, pimps and dodgers, tramps and whores and twaddlers, of their vices and their lingo, all of this would have brought him among the most prominent authors of his nation; he would have been called "Maestro", in a foretaste of national funerals and posthumous statues. He preferred to stay in the shadows instead, and pull the strings from backstage with artfulness beyond compare. Judging by the way he manipulated people and situations, how he fooled and confused them all, young and old, while never once falling at a loss himself, you might say he was a true juggling prodigy. He would con and fool and scam the whole neighbourhood, have them all dance to his delirious music, just like he had the three of us sucked into his crazy puppet show, whirling and tossing us about with little care if we stood or fell. It was hard to find a lower, sleazier, more treacherous villain on earth—or again, a more propitious guide for the third excursion of the day, a crude passage from life as fancy into life as hard reality. And yet, many times I thought I was simply dreaming it all then.

No sooner had we finished dining than Pirgu was on his way out. The man was thirsty. The place was lavish with Bordeaux and Bourgogne wines, inexpensive and more than enough to supply a royal feast. Such stuff would not appeal to Gorică though, who preferred the lighter choice of domestic wines. He returned with the glorious news of having spotted something to the best of his taste and dragged us along to some God-forsaken slum, only to offend our palate with a thick rancid slop he called wine. Like a veritable sea wolf, Pantazi would gulp down whatever came to his mouth, even more readily so than Pașadia, who did not care as much for a drink as for a brilliant banquet bustle.

But we soon stood up and left further on the quest as Pirgu suddenly recalled a fabulous free-run grape juice not to be missed at the Raised Porch, or a hare-blood red wine to make you lick your lips with delight. From one tavern to the next we stopped at Proțăpeasca's[83] or Pepi Şmarot's for a coffee and a chat with the girls over a glass of something, while Pirgu was making some arrangement for Paşadia or someone else for the next day. We then sometimes made a short call up at the "club", where Paşadia would strike a few tentative bets at chemin-de-fer. This was not a regular call though, as women and card playing were subjects to be addressed in the hours before supper.

It wasn't before the third station[84] that the orgy rose to its peak, wild and fierce like hell itself. The sentries of the nightly shore were fidgeting and fretting and fussing about us in a sinister masquerade in the whirling of which Gorică let himself go free, at the peak of elation and excitement. Like quicksilver he would sweep from one table to the next, squeezing roars of laughter round the place; he was the yeast and the heart of the party; he told the musicians what to play, he would treat them to drinking rounds, would kiss them smack on the lips and then curse and slap them in the face. In fact, it was not unusual for the whole thing to end up in a general brawling bustle toward the early morning hours. Perfectly ignorant of the savagely rising ruckus around them, as if miles away, Pantazi and Paşadia remained absorbed in their remote contemplation. On the contrary, they looked as if

83 Proțăpeasca [protsə'pæska] is the feminine for Proțăpescu, a less common and rather funny Romanian family name.

84 The Third Station is a likely allusion to the place on Via Dolorosa where Jesus Christ falls for the first time under the weight of the cross. The author may have resorted to such an extreme metaphor to emphasise the staggering effect of extreme sinful passion and debauchery on the original purity of the human soul.

peace and quiet had been the truly hostile medium to disrupt their reverie. Just as strange, whenever Pirgu was not with us—either out scheming and hustling, or loitering over a card game with Mehtupciu[85]—and we attended, in his absence, such joints as he had introduced us to, we would be just sitting there staring blankly at the glasses in front, flat and listless to whatever stood or moved around us. Indeed we could make little of the night life if he wasn't there to kindle the scene; for he was the fascinating epitome of Bucharest's underground dregs. That was why we followed suit in his steps, in the mud and the sleet and the slush of sloppy, rutted, nameless back lanes at the end of town and across filthy vacant lots littered with trash and foul, stinking carcasses; we entered, almost on all fours, into those stuffy mud-floored shanty homes, painted in colours as loud as the yellow or red rags of bare-footed gypsy women who would lie down to the next butcher or tripe man for small change, a shot of cheap brandy or a pack of tobacco. While visiting no families, we managed to fall even deeper... The next halt was the market place, where we would linger over a tripe soup, in anticipation of the break of day. Oh, for the daybreak...

...Pașadia suddenly bristled and his mood turned sour, as if he was trying to shake off the memory of a nightmare. I averted my eyes from his stern, bitter face in those moments; I couldn't bear to see his hazy stare, telling of agonising dismay. His murderous ancestor must have felt a like urgency to

---

85 Most probably a nickname, based on the Turkish mektupçu, meaning a clerk in a chancellor's office.

go into hiding before daylight came to shine on him. We would eventually separate for the day, dragging our spent carcasses each his own way. While Paşadia and Pantazi headed straight home, I went for a steam bath and Pirgu called on the midwife for a massage with rose vinegar and opodeldoc[86]. His eccentricities had by now become a familiar show in the slum of Jarcaleţi where he lived with his parents, and the neighbourhood were hardly surprised to see him come home in the morning with two barrel organs each playing a different tune, or with a dancing bear[87], a group of *Căluş* dancers[88] or *Paparude*[89], or riding a water waggon or a hearse, or lying on a stretcher.

Our wanton debauchery, deplorable though it was, had not been for nothing—be it only for the noble friendship that bloomed and ripened between Pantazi and Paşadia. To my mind, more than the erudition and the courtesy they had in common, it was their melancholy that drew them together. However, while with the former you could speak of a mild

86 A liniment consisting of a mixture of soap in alcohol, camphor, and herbal essences.

87 A tamed bear trained to dance for the spectators' entertainment.

88 Căluş [ka'loosh] is the name of an old traditional folk dance in several parts of Romania. Performed only by men dressed in richly coloured, most attractive popular costumes, the Căluş is a very dynamic group dance that requires hard training and dedication.

89 Paparude used to be women dancers wrapped in green leafage round their naked bodies (or sometimes just rags) who would perform a ritual dance to conjure the rain in dry weather (approx. rainwomen).

nostalgia as if in blue reminiscence of the good old days, the latter was rather a case of dark, ultimate despair. Since it was Pantazi who more often than not assumed the bill for our evening repasts, rejecting the slightest tentative offer from Paşadia, the latter resolved to feast him in return and made an invitation to his place. For the first time, the cupboards and chests produced the Holland table cloth, the Bohemian china dishware and crystal glasses, and the gold-plated silverware. The dining room was richly decorated with yellow roses that gained a waxen translucence in the lingering amber light of that last silky autumn afternoon of the year. I felt so far away from Bucharest, and I felt as if it were a feast to celebrate Paşadia's abdication of his escapades with Pirgu, who had declined the invitation for that day.

After dinner we were ushered into a chamber deco-rated in the most precious Vienna Rococo style, the walls and furniture all lined in saffron silk dotted with silver tinfoil shaped as water lilies. We called it Kaunitz'[90] Salon, after a pompous portrait of the prince-chancellor wearing the Golden Fleece cloak, and also because the place had been designed as a replica of a drawing room in his old Gartenpa-last in Mariahilf. All that refined, aristocratic setting was so much in resonance with Paşadia's substance and spirit. In him, the scholar and the philosopher had been grafted onto a grim, hateful bailiff eager to show his horns and cloven hoof in the company of his like. Pantazi stood in perplexed admi-ration for the mark of noble dignity in the man's poise and bearing, the perfect control of motion and rhetoric, or his bit-

---

90 Wenzel Anton Kaunitz (1711-1794) was an Austrian diplomat and chancellor whose palace (Gartenpalast) was located in Mariahilferstrasse, in Vienna.

ter sarcasm, colder than ice, sharper than a steel blade and more vicious than poison. How he ever came to acquire all those qualities is still beyond my comprehension; for it is true that, while taking generations to foster, heredity is definitely written in the blood. So where did he get that sterling drop of the purest blue which bloomed so glorious in him, in defiance of the tainted streaks that came with crossbreeding? What secret kinship did he have with those venerable figures of the past whose portraits he liked to have around and whose con-tumacies, vices and tastes he shared to such a point that, had they come to life again, they would see more similitude in him than in their own descendants? But it was then that I un-derstood why he had been called out "raca"[91], and I realised what an unearthly, frightening monster he must have looked in the eyes of that society of confused freshly freed serfs, of rogues and dodgers, all of whom came down on him to sweep him out of existence.

As the evening crept in and conversation was fading, my mind was mulling over all the gossip I had heard about Paşadia. His abrupt passage from utter poverty to vast wealth was even now, many years on, rich food for speculation: ei-ther he must be in the service of some foreign power, or he was being paid the price of silence over who knows what dire information he might possess... After all, except for the real estate in which he had invested bucketfuls of money, there

---

91 An offensive appellation in Hebrew meaning an idiot or a fool, indicating utter contempt and anathema. Contempt was a very serious sin liable to the judgement of the Sanhedrin, the supreme court of the Jews (see The Gospel according to Matthew, 5: 21-2).

was no tangible wealth or source of income one could attach to his name, and neither was he a brigand or a forger like his grandfather—but then, who knows... There was also a story putting his wealth down to the cavalry commander: from the faraway country he was hiding in under some different name, rich and lonely and feeling his end was near, the old man had summoned his grandson to bestow his riches on him.

True, the intricate chronicle of my friend's life had many missing pages, as he had vanished out of sight so many years that people had come to think he was dead. The elaborate secrecy he chose to weave about himself had sent rumours spinning about: in his secluded quarters surrounded by gardens he kept, they said, either in hiding or locked up, a woman—a woman who was not quite in her right mind; sometimes, at night, screams could be heard coming from that place, they said. Then, a dramatic incident in Bucharest's mundane life—the dubious suicide of a fairly well known personage whose wife was said to be entertaining an affair with Paşadia—made the talk of the town soar to fever peak: caught red-handed, they said, he hadn't hesitated to add one more blood-smeared link to his forefathers' long chain of abominations.

This kind of stories, had they been sworn to be the truth, the whole truth and nothing by the truth, failed to stir the faintest shade of my interest. What I was truly curious about was a certain detail that had escaped everybody else's attention: Paşadia would often say he was taking a few days' leave to the mountains; but nobody knew, or at least won-

dered, what that secret Horeb[92] was whence he always returned refreshed and invigorated. I could have naturally pre-
sumed that, after long weeks of sleepless nights, this incredibly sturdy fellow was seeking peace and comfort in the brisk,
fresh air and the deep solitude of the highlands; and I would
have contented myself with this surmise, had I not heard an
aunt of mine, an elderly lady who was a far-off relative of
Paşadia's, say that he sometimes was seized with terrifying
fits of rage but, as he felt them coming, he would seclude and
lock himself up until they were gone. With whatever else I
knew, this intimation had produced in my mind a string of
associations that I feared to even give a second thought.

When I left the place with Pantazi, a strange thought
occurred to me for the first time: though I had come to feel
this man as an age-old friend, sometimes almost an alter-ego,
I didn't even know his real name! In fact, the initial letter of
the name he was generally known by was missing from the
embroidered monogram on some of his belongings. However, it was far less than could baffle my feelings, for the
privilege of enjoying the company of two unique, as they
were strange, individuals, was added to the absolute thrill of
moving around two mysteries which, if faced with each-other
like mirrors, would undoubtedly reflect ad infinitum. I was
only wondering if I would ever have the chance to get to
know at least a tiny part of any of them.

---

92 A mountain in the Sinai Peninsula which the Book of Deuteronomy in the Holy Bible
reports to be the place where Moses received the Ten Commandments from God.

Confessions

...sage citoyen du vaste univers.[93]

La Fontaine[94]

Pirgu had left in the direction of the Post Office, while we made for Sărindar[95]. The fog was thickening, the humid air was bone-chilling. We stepped into the nearest bistro, Durieu's, right behind the National Bank, and we picked the far corner table. That evening, my friend looked somewhat under the weather: he was not in the mood to tell a story, drink or smoke; he was sighing profusely and rubbing his eyes. After the strange delight he had taken, hardly an hour before, in Pena's no less strange vituperation, he had, again as strangely, sunk into a state of bleak dejection. So woe-begone had I never seen him before, so I watched him discreetly, knowing that what usually brings comfort in such moments is confession. I felt he was not far from it, and I was

---

93 In French: wise citizen of the vast universe.

94 Jean de la Fontaine (1621-1695), the most popular French poet and fable author of the 17th century.

95 Formerly a square in the centre of Bucharest.

not wrong: after he came to himself a little, he began to speak in a faltering voice:

'I owe you some explanation, my friend. You might have thought it queer that I haven't as yet told you who I am; I beg for your pardon, it was not my intention. For the sake of such unrestrained affection as you have shown me I decided, from the very early moments of our acquaintance, to break my resolve of remaining "incognito" for as long as I walk my shadow around this part of the world; and if I haven't done it yet, it was only in expectation of a favourable moment. There were so many other things to recount! In your presence I enjoyed recalling thirty years of travelling, and still in your presence I will, if it doesn't bother you, revisit my childhood and my early youth tonight.

'To begin with, I must say Bucharest was the place where I opened my eyes upon this world; more precisely, my parents' house stood on Earthen Bridge[96], across from Viişoara. However, I am of foreign descent,' he continued with a perceptibly patronising pitch. 'Yes, I am a Greek of noble Mediterranean blood; I traced my forefathers back to the sixteenth century: free men, valiant pirates streaking the high seas for loot and plunder, from Jaffa to the Balearic Islands and from Ragusa to Tripoli. My lineage descends along one of two branches out of Zuani the Red, through two sons of his. When he hosted me once at his palace in Catania, the

---

96 Today contained well within the city, Earthen Bridge (in Romanian, Podul de Pământ) used to be a sloppy, rutted road at the edge of Bucharest, following the course of the Dambovitsa River. In 1878 it was renamed Plevna Road (in Romanian, Calea Plevnei), in memory of the victorious Romanian troops against the Turks at Plevna, Bulgaria, in 1877.

head of the Sicilian branch boasted—and tried to convince me—of our barbaric origin. He belonged to the so-called 'Panther branch' because, to honour an illustrious matrimonial alliance, he had added to the original coat of arms (which featured a red arrow piercing the neck of a silver swan in flight against a blue field, all that on a shield sustained by unicorns) a black panther against a golden field framed in marten skin. Of Norman origin we may well be, since all of them down to the last two—he and I, that is—have been marked with the indelible brand of the race: red hair and blue eyes. In any case, there is no doubt I come of a seed of seamen, and this is my only streak of vanity, for if I were to choose my forebears, as there is the custom with some pretended blue-bloods, I would still search for a shipman at the top of the ladder. I would like to be a descendant of Thamus[97], the sailor who heard a heavenly voice carried by the gentle evening breeze to order him to take the news of the demise of the great Pan. Indeed there is nothing else I pride myself upon, not even the blood my people shed under the battle flags of the Heteria[98], those in the Swan branch, who then fled Candia through Fanar into Russia and on to the Romanian provinces.

---

97 Pan, the god of shepherds and flocks, and Asklepios, the god of medicine, are the only gods that Greek mythology reports to have died. During the reign of Tiberius (A.D. 14–37), Thamus, a sailor on his way to Italy, heard an ethereal voice calling him across the sea: "Thamus, are you there? When you reach Palodes, take care to proclaim that the great god Pan is dead." (See also Plutarch, De defectu Oraculorum ("The Obsolescence of Oracles").

98 A secret society during the Greek revolution of 1821.

'On the other hand, while I am not exactly proud of my ancestors, they have every reason to be proud of me, as my avatar has been the epitome of their generosity and enterprise, their spirit of sacrifice, their propensity for greatness, and that ineffable, inherent seduction that made them take root and indurate wherever fate pleased to blow their seed. And this, I think, was because my blood is not the issue of conflicting bloodlines: my parents were close kin, they were cousins-german. Almost level in age, both orphaned, they had been raised together and it didn't take long before they took to each-other. In the long run, against all prejudice, their romance was consecrated in marriage.

'I was an only child; they loved me with all their living love, I was the mirror of their twin souls melted to make one, almost a victim of their overwhelming care. Thank God, the milk I sucked did not come from a strange bosom, either. All in all, my childhood was a carefree, blessed, happy time. And every time I think of it, it's like I see the sweep of white doves against the clear blue sky on a springtime morning. Among my recollections, this is the earliest—a symbolic piece of memory, too.

'But the child, much as he was cuddled and pampered, was far from a light-hearted, lively piece of flesh. My soul was always clouded with that hazy melancholy mood of an oversensitive nature, reluctant even to a tender stroke, or a perceptible source of pleasure. Long before I read any of Lucretius, I had sensed that sensuousness unharnessed was inevitably followed by a bitter sense

'I don't think there are many whom life and age have changed so little as they have me. I'll be the same till the day

I die: a devoted dreamer, forever lured by the remote and the mysterious. I remember the days when, as a child, I forgot about playing and sneaked into the garden to listen, from behind the fence, to a woman lisping in a weak voice: "A bird in the tree, joyous and free, I come in tears o'er my misery…" and then she crumbled in long, heartrending sobs. After a while, the chant was gone. Yes, and when evening came, I liked to sit down on the porch beside Osman the dog and watch the sky filling out with stars.

'Possibly one more sign that I am getting old, now that I have returned to the cradle of my early years: such memories of the good old days keep coming back on me with uncanny clarity, sometimes to the brink of hallucination. As it once happened in Cişmegiu Park, I had a real, palpable vision of myself as a small child, fifty years ago, when Mama Sia would hold my hand as we strolled under those same trees.

'Next to my parents, good old Mama Sia has her place in my heart. She had first been theirs and then my nanny, a most trustworthy woman who brought us all up. She was looked upon as a relative of ours, and there were muffled rumours that she even was one. She received no pay, had her seat round the table beside us and she called our names and talked to us in the most familiar way, she was grumbling and picking on the lot of us as if she was the true master of the house—which in fact she was, for my mother was completely carefree and careless about the place.

'My mother was more like a doll—the sweetest, loveliest doll on the face of the earth to me. To see her letting down her rich long hair like auburn honey, and to cross her deep blue gaze under dark eyebrows, you might have said that she was one of those pure Magdalenes painted in the tender days of Italian decadence, who had just stepped out of the frame, alive. I loved her to adoration, but I still feel I didn't love her enough, and the thought of it brings me to despair.

'With my father, it was different. My feeling for him was closer to reason and sprang from admiration. The graceful gentleman with effeminate hands who had been taken for an Englishman in Paris, by his genteel manners and appearance, had revealed rare virtues that crowned a true character. His scholarly education and the protection he enjoyed from Voivode Alexandru Ioan[99] eased his way to an appointment at the Court of Appeals, soon after to be promoted at the High Court of Justice. Then he went into Parliament. He can be credited with having had a great say in the impropriation of monastic assets and the land reform in favour of the peasantry. He was the youngest, if not the most outstanding, of the several reputable figures who stepped down from politics for ever after Voivode Cuza was relegated. I was already in my teens when, one afternoon, two unknown boyars visited my father and they sat talking in the drawing room for more

---

99 Alexandru Ioan Cuza authored the unification of the Principalities of Wallachia and Moldavia (1859) into a single country which was formally declared three years later, in 1862, under the name of Romania. The unification was completed at the end of World War II with the third province, Transylvania. A prominent figure in Romanian history, Cuza passed a number of bills that revolutionised the social, economic and political life of the country.

than an hour. Toward the end of the conversation my father left them alone for a while and went into my mother's boudoir. He returned shortly to see the guests off to their carriage. In the evening of that day I learned that my father had asked my mother's consent for his declining a minister's position in the government. In fact, my father would never fail to consult my mother before taking a decision, if only to avoid the slightest ruffle in the peace and quiet of our home-sweet-home—something which was not, however, devoid of all inconvenience. Although we were comfortably well-off, our lifestyle was far below our possibilities. We could have lived in grand style, but my mother simply dreaded the slightest change: she would never, for the world, leave Bucharest for a travel to the countryside, to the vineyard, or to a spa. And, come to think of it, what an excitement a wagon journey must have been to Borsec, or Zaizon… She was even slow to leave the house. Who would have thought she was ever going to give birth to a progeny who was to compass the earth more than once!

'Poor mother, she was overwhelmed with most of what the world had in stock. She suffered from cold like no one I've known, and from heat no less. She kept away from sunshine as much as wind; light was aggressive, night was oppressive, and the slightest noise made her start; if she saw blood she fainted on the spot; receptions and soirees were such a time of weariness and tedium for her—and oh, was she celebrated! A company of her own condition she didn't care to entertain; instead, she herded daily a garrulous host of prying purlieu pauper petticoats, priests' wives, midwives, confectioners, fortune tellers, the lot. It was her pleasure to dress up country-folk style, with skirts richly folded at the waist and parted at the front, a kerchief on her head, and she wore necklaces of coral or silver coins. And she confessed, in all honesty, that she enjoyed the fiddlers' music more than the Italian opera. "Anicuța[100] is looking the wrong way," my aunt Smaranda used to say about my mother. When aunt Smaranda died we inherited all of her real estate at the Red Fount[101], but it was still my mother who put her foot down against our moving on to that property: she said Earthen Bridge was a much nicer place to stay. And maybe she was right. All the way from St. Constantin's to St. Elefterie's[102], and from Giafer's pothouse garden down to Pricopoaia's house, an abandoned place of derelict ruins these days, there used to be rows of gardens overflowing with flowers and fruit trees, lilac and vine arbours; camomile and mallows invaded the yards; a profusion of laurels, pomegranates and thyme, and the window sills were lined with carnations, geraniums, fuchsia, sweet peas, or gillyflowers. And over in the distance, across the river, the hazy green vision of Cotroceni Hill raised the skyline...'

My friend paused with a smile, took his time lighting a cigarette, then ordered coffee and wine before resuming his account.

---

100 A diminutive for Ana.

101 In 19th c. Bucharest, Cişmeaua Roşie (the Red Fount) was an indigent precinct round Mogoşoaia Bridge (today's Victoria Avenue, Calea Victoriei), marked by a public fountain. Incidentally, it was the place where the first theatre in Bucharest was founded by Princess Ralu, daughter to Voivode Ioan Gheorghe Caragea. It was here that the local audience could for the first time attend Schiller's Robbers, Goethe's Faust, or Lessing's Emilia Galotti.

102 Local Orthodox churches.

'In a brightly lit salon, stately matrons dressed in sumptuous hoop skirts and laden with jewellery, and whiskered boyars, pendants with shiny brilliant stones hanging from their necks, are bowing in deep reverence to kiss the hand of an old shrunken lady dressed in green, her hair dyed a shade of carrot, her eyes a hazy blue. But the old lady stands above her decrepitude: upright in a majestic pose, her head raised, her look lofty and piercing, her speech clear, terse, imperative. After her last journey to Baden-Baden she had never left the house again, and because loneliness was unbearable and sleep was scarce, she entertained a live company into the late hours each night after a copious supper of twelve round the table.

'She was one of the lingering remnants of a golden age: she died in 1871, going on eighty-eight, a widow for seventy-two years, after a short marriage with a Greek prince, a voracious youngster who had died of a volvulus after glutting himself with blueberries. She would never marry again, and lived the rest of her long life inside the cocoon of aristocratic prejudice, which she held in reverence with fanatic ardour. However, her presumptuous pose was fully forgiven and forgotten the moment you heard her speak, as her rhetoric was even more impressive than her prodigious memory: indeed, she had a unique way of telling about the tiniest trifle, and whenever she spoke you could be forgiven for thinking she was reading from a beautiful book. Other than that, she was the epitome of common sense: no quirks and twists with her, no fancy superstitions—even the only disputable idiosyncrasy of always wearing green and never displaying another stone but emeralds had not been her own choice to make. With time the green darkened under the flimsy cover of a black lacework veil, and it was not before she lay in her coffin that she was once more clad, as she had requested, in the orange silk dress she had worn on her wedding day.

'May her soul rest in peace! My gratitude to her weighs no less than a creed. Apart from substantial assets, she passed down to me the sacred legacy of tradition, as she is the one to have truly fashioned my spirit: while guiding my steps toward elevation of thought, she awakened in me ancestral aspirations. It is from her that I learned I belonged in that privileged caste destined by God to command, those whom wealth and fame raises above the condition of common mortals. As for the dire moments that prompted the course of my later life, she was always present at the back of my mind to steer my decisions: when ridden with doubt and apprehension, her radiant apparition was always there, in perfect serenity, dressed in her green garb and shining with green emeralds from top to toe.

'Every afternoon I was taken to her place, and I sat there watching how she adorned herself, which usually took until evening. All this time she never stopped talking. She had mingled with the rank and fashion of nearly two generations: she had seen Napoleon I a few times, he had even spoken to her once; she had been to Vienna with her father during the days of the Congress[103] and danced with Emperor Alexander and Metternich; in Italy, Chateaubriand and Byron had paid their respects to her. For fear she might lose the

---

103 The Congress of Vienna was held from September 1814 till June 1815, after the Napoleonic Wars, to the end of revamping the balance of power across Europe among Great Britain, Russia, Austria and Prussia.

caimacam's[104] major-general pension, which had been extended to her by order of Emperor Nicholas, she never went to France again since 1830; in fact, after the ungodly Crimean War, as she used to call it, she hated France like poison. However, the next language she cherished the most after Greek was French—that stylish elite idiom spoken at the Court of France, so rich and colourful, spirited and spicy, somehow redolent of bergamot pears and musk. But when she slipped into some episode about our ancestors, her tongue turned Romanian and her account was bathed in a mystic light as the words entwined in a sublime symphony telling about the stubborn struggle against the pagan invaders, about relentless sacrifice, about piety and devotion overpowering the frigid fangs of fate.

'So passionate was she as she spoke about the betrayals of the two chief dragomans and their bitter atonement, and about the other heads, eight by the count, fallen under the scimitar in less than a hundred years; about the flight to Russia, the fomentation of two wars and the rise of the Heteria. Nothing could enchant me more than those stories; and the greater pleasure came with the account of her recollections from her long-gone childhood, so remote as it had been a blissful time, replete with lavish delight and fondness. The old lady whom I was watching in the mirror while she bedecked herself among candles lit ahead of dusk had been one of three gems that bled so many hearts. In a dreamlike vision I contemplated the three of them, arms round one-another's waist, young, fair, blue-eyed, dark-browed: Bălaşa, Zamfira

---

104 In former Moldova and Wallachia, a caimacam (or kaymakam, a word of Turkish origin) was the voivode's minister, or sub-governor.

and Smaranda. Their mother, Păuna, the caimacam's wife, had baptized each in dedication to one patron gem to blow wind in their sails and had sworn them to wear the colour of that single stone for as long as they lived[105].

'You'd say it all sounds like a fairy tale, wouldn't you? In fact, it's only a tiny detail from the fabulous biography of that princess of all favours, my great-grandmother. Some day I'll give you the whole story, and then you might be surprised to see that our genteel tastes and trivial vanities, our attraction to flowers and flavours, adornments and jewellery, our appetency for a leisurely, affluent life have come down to us from her along the Romanian, rather than the Greek, descendence. Her fairness, too, was added to the lot. Eager to discover from whom I had inherited these peculiar inclinations of my nature, I delved into the family history for the particulars of my ancestors; since records were scarce, however, the old lady was nearly the only source for my study, which was far less than enough to trace back the strangest idiosyncrasy of my personality. You must have noticed my irresistible soft spot for gypsies, how deeply their wretched fate affects me, and how happy I am to converse with them in their much despised vernacular. This I acquired as a small child at the cookhouse, from Uncle Stan the aspic maker, grown grey and all but blind. He would not avail himself of the Manumission Act[106] to leave our household, the

---

105 The names Bălaşa, Zamfira, Smaranda are resonant of amber, sapphire, and emerald, respectively.

106 On the 20th of February 1856, during the reign of Alexandru Ioan Cuza, the Manumission Act was passed, by which gypsies were officially freed from serfdom and ransomed by

place where he had been born, and stayed to die there. With his eyesight he had lost his sleep too, and he sat by the hearth, pipe in mouth, day or night, winter or summer. He loved me like nothing else in the world; when I was fever-ish—for I used to get the evil eye so easily, to the dismay of everybody in the house—I remember him taking me in his arms, cuddling and rocking me gently. And there are many other gypsy faces rising from the past in my memory, giving me their friendly grin, with flashy white teeth. It was a gypsy woman who introduced me into manhood—a gypsy woman against the wall… She was wearing a red flower behind her ear and danced as she walked. I was sixteen then. It happened one evening in the acacia season, and the rain had barely stopped. I gave her a gold coin and forgot to ask her name. And I've never met her since…'

And so he kept on spinning tales about this and that, from which I gathered that he had received a most meticulous education and enjoyed the fruit of thorough studies under the purposeful guidance of his enlightened father, who was plan-ning to send him to some distinguished school in Paris; but he met the allied opposition of madam Anicuța and Sia. After all, his own heart sank at the thought of having to leave be-hind such a pair of loving parents who treated him as if they had been his elder brother and sister—which in fact their ap-pearance even looked like, some years later. He might have stayed with them to live that cosy peaceful life forever if the war hadn't broken out in 1877, just when he had turned twenty. But let him take the floor again.

---

the state. Many of them, however, had become attached to their patrons' families and would not leave.

'I went to inform my father of my firm determination to join the army, a decision I was determined to defend against the whole world. The great Alexander Nikolaevich, the Orthodox czar, had drawn his sword against the invader, and from that day there could be no greater honour for me, dead or alive, than under the banners of the Holy Eastern Empire. My father was truly apprehensive of my mother's response—and you can but imagine his stupefaction when I told him I had her permission, as she had been the first to hear of my resolve. What happened in her heart then will forever be a mystery to me. And the miracle—for it appeared as nothing less to my mind—went further than that, as the angel doll had turned into a full-fledged matron overnight. She opened the Red Fount estate, made it into a hospital for the wounded and managed it to the best of her knowledge and abilities, so adeptly that you might have said she had been doing it for a lifetime. For his part, my father received a commission with Prince Gortchakoff[107], whose family had fostered friendly ties with ours. I, too, enjoyed the camaraderie of even higher royalty, proven and confirmed on the battlefield—Sergej Leuchtenberg, you will remember I mentioned his name. Oh, had he been alive now... His death, to which I was a close witness, marked the beginning of an agonising train of afflictions for me. I returned home only to learn that my mother had gone. Like all of her family, she had spared herself no pains. Stricken with a heavy cold in the dire winter of the war, she had refused to tend to herself and

---

107 Alexander Gortchakoff (1798-1883) was a Russian politican and diplomat, ambassador to Stuttgart and Vienna, then foreign minister (1856); he opposed Bismarck and fervently championed Pan-Slavism.

stood in haughty fortitude under the pangs of the malady. Far away from husband and son, at the end of her tether, she had peacefully breathed her last in Mama Sia's arms, with no murmur or tear. Some of the braves whose pains she had soothed wept as they carried the coffin on their shoulders. The horrors of the war had somewhat hardened me against this blow which, instead, was devastating to my father. I had come to the point that knowing her dead was often less painful than seeing him alive. Raw-boned, sunken shoulders, long, grey, unkempt hair and beard, untrimmed dirty nails, sloppy and slimy from head to toe, the poor man had gone beyond recognition. Even as he didn't speak, his glazed eyes spelt utter despondency and a waning intellect. His domestic tragedy only added to the deep distress he had felt upon the loss of Bessarabia[108]: if I hadn't been quick to discover, he would have sent back the St. Ana Cordon, the fifth out of six decorations bestowed to honour our house. It was not long before I realised it was hopeless: the man was doomed. He went without food or sleep, headlong into brandy and tobacco. A few months later he came to rest by my mother's side. Mama Sia would soon take her place at their feet—and there I was, all alone in the world.

'It did take time before I pulled myself together. I rarely left my quarters, and it was not before much later that I began to go on horseback outings; and as I crossed the bridge

---

108 The eastern part of the former Principality of Moldavia, between the rivers Prut and Dniester; a land of long and bitter dispute between Russia and Romania, Bessarabia ended up as what is known today as the Republic of Moldova. The population are still of Romanian descent in their majority, as is the toponymy.

at "Marmizon"[109], a fair demoiselle would often cross my path. Her appearance had so much grown into a pattern that after a while I grew anxious, with every tour, that I might not see her there—and when it so happened, I felt miserable. The innocent pleasure to see her soon turned into a sort of tender anticipation. Day or night, her face was floating behind my brow, and I couldn't separate the thought of her from an irresistible feeling of excitement; when I saw her in the flesh I almost swooned in awkward bashfulness of the kind I had never felt before. In fact, it was the very reason why I wasn't able to break the word to her for quite some time. The strange feeling I had about this interlude was not so much due to the fact that I had fallen in love—after all, I was in line for it—as it was to the very object of my passion; for as far as I knew, mine was the swarthy type, the darker the better—and she was as blonde and pale-skinned as you'll ever meet. It should then be of no surprise to you, my friend, if I say I truly loved her with all my heart, while her tangible presence, even close, failed to stir the deepermost ferment of my manly nature. In fact, the secret spring of my attachment to her was sheer sympathy.

'Wanda—that was the girl's name—had told me, all in tears, about her wretched life in the house of her father, a drunkard of a Polack who lived from hand to mouth on what little he earned mending clothes and cleaning spots, and his wicked second wife. She said they were trying to sell her away, as they had done with her elder sister. Upon her dis-

---

109 A popular distortion of Malmaison, the name originally given by Voivode Alexandru Ioan Cuza to the military location where a consistent cavalry corps had been quartered to stand in defence of the city of Bucharest.

tressing confession I decided to save her, to shake off all prejudice and raise her to the dignity of my position. While well aware of the public scandal I was in for, it was not the rebuke of the living I feared the most, but rather that of my dead ancestors, whose censure I could not spurn as freely, and there were chilling sleepless nights when they appeared before my eyes, lined up against a red-gold background like in the old Greek icons, stiff in their gold-lined brocade caftans, those haughty archons holding their severed heads in their hands, their eyes looking away in disdain from the renegade that I was. However, I was too weak to turn back on my decision, so I let myself carried by the winds of fate. The wedding day drew nearer as the year was dragging to its bleak end; I had even ordered the rings. The very day I brought them home from the jeweller's, complete with our names engraved, I found Madame Elenca, the bailiff's wife, one of the more trustworthy gossipmongers of my mother's company, sitting on the bench outside the gate, with news for me. At the time I was still living on Earthen Bridge—Plevna Road, as they call it today. With an indefinite feeling of apprehension, I invited her in. After a mournful introduction on Madame Anicuța, she presently dried her tears and proceeded with a disparaging lecture as to what a huge mistake I was going to make, even if Wanda had been an honest lass and not a despicable wench who had lain with the basest of rogues and scoundrels and was no stranger to the doctor or the midwife. I was absolutely stupefied. "If you don't believe me, my dear boy," she added, "then why don't you lay wait after eleven hours in the night and see for yourself how she brings in her stud through the window. And let me tell you who he is: Fane the widow's son, the bloke with the accordion."

'I felt a pang in my heart, my ears began to ring, the house spinning around me. It was a deadly blow. But as the most desperate plight was less than could get the better of my judgment, I managed once more to stay in the light of cold reason. She might well have gone wrong before knowing me, the more as she had lived in want of protection and fair guidance—that much I could understand, painful though it was; but to taint my reputation so boorishly, and only days before our wedding—that was beyond all pardonable bounds. Then I remembered, when my mother once had my future told, I learned my life course was written in for all blessings, save the one of true love. So I gave my thanks to Madame Elenca and told her to go in peace. When Wanda came, as usual, around noon, she found me all dressed up for departure, fastening the belts round my suitcase: an urgent trip to the countryside for a few days, I told her. Her countenance gave away nothing but infinite purity and tenderness. I was suddenly stricken with the agony of doubt, the most torturous of all torments, for I couldn't possibly get the notion of this dainty creature ignoring so recklessly the brightest of luck that one of her kind and position could have ever dreamt of.

'We left together in the same carriage; I dropped her at her place and continued along Cotroceni Road, made a tour of the whole city and at dusk I returned to the Red Fount via Bridge-End[110]. I stepped into the long-forsaken chapel, where I hadn't set foot since boyhood; I lit a torch wick left from the days of old and, conjuring the spirit of Princess Smaranda to intercede with the Holy Ghost in my favour, I sank into prayer.

---

110 In the original: Capu Podului (literally, the End of the Bridge).

'The Heavenly Grace wasn't long to enlighten me, and so I realised that whatever was coming upon me was to the benefit of my own salvation, while Wanda was either to be proved unfaithful, or otherwise disappear altogether. For God would not endure the emblem of our house to be tainted after it had, since 1812, been lavishly displayed below an earl's crown against the chest of the Russian two-headed eagle. And then I muttered: "Not ours, Lord, but Your blessed name may shine in eternal glory!" I was seized by an intense feeling of horror at the thought of the deadly trap I had been just going to step into. I left the chapel calm and composed, at peace with my fate. The dire thoughts I had mulled over along the way were replaced by fear lest the bailiff's wife should have told me less than the truth; but two hours later I found sweet comfort in the painful confirmation of treachery. Now that the creature who had nested my youthful dream of love was lost to me, I decided that all I had left to do was to put her out of my mind altogether.

'But I couldn't possibly do it. Even today, thirty years later, my feeling for her hasn't faded; instead, distance and time have turned her into a mystical presence: it is not the personal Wanda I love, not her flesh-and-blood appearance which, if still alive, must be now a withered, worn-out frame, but my own tender memories of her. As for the women who have since crossed my path, all I loved about them was some detail reminding me of her: the blond curls or the green eyes with some, the melancholy smile, the waddle or the entrancing voice with others... This is why I agreed with Paşadia the other day, when he said he saw nothing in love but fetishism. Yes, fetishism, fetishism...'

He shrugged and disposed of the cigarette that had burnt itself out, ash intact, neglected all through the account. He ordered fruit, a stronger wine and another round of coffee. He tasted, then sipped, then resumed his tale.

'To divert myself, I plunged into a life of dissipation with boundless impetus, so that the whole city was stunned in the face of such ultimate debauchery. For one whole year the orgies ran all through the night into broad daylight at the Red Fount, where I had moved my lodging. A copious company orbed around me in a display of the most depraved mores of Bucharest society. When I went hunting or made a tour round the monasteries there was always a cortege of at least twenty carriages, all full, plus the domestics in charge of provisions and refreshments, and my band of musicians. True, there was never once the slightest fault I could find, and everybody was doing the best of their best to pamper me, sometimes even to excess: it was enough, for instance, to declare my appreciation for this or that woman to find her in my bed in the evening. There were husbands and brothers who even brought me their own wives or sisters. But I was so wastefully extravagant to stand up to such a prodigal spending spree that, after all my cash inheritance had been wasted, I plunged into debt as recklessly as you might ever imagine. And every time I hit rock bottom I ran to uncle Scarlat, alias "Kettle", an old rascal of a boyar, a middleman, horse dealer and you may guess what more, and he would presently come up with a loan at downright savage interest. So I came to sink deeper and deeper. When my earnings were due, the leases and rents went to cover my bills of exchange which, of course, I had to accept. Then I had to endorse more bills—and so I signed on, sometimes not fully aware of what I signed, until one morning when I sent uncle Scarlat for more and he came back empty-handed, telling me the purse was dry and I would soon have to clear the whole account. With a broad sneer, he advised me to sell whatever I owned before they came to repossess in force. He even offered to find buyers for me. Instead, I sent him out and urged him to come up with some silver: it was the eve of my birthday and, for some definite purpose, I wanted to give a handsome party. I gave him some buckles and girdles of lady Smaranda's paraphernalia to put in pawn.

"I was indeed fortunate," he said as he came back with good money. "My friend was leaving Bucharest, and a quarter of an hour later would have been too late."

'Again, I didn't ask who that mysterious pawnbroker was: what business was it of mine, after all? I charged uncle Scarlat with the due preparations and invitations for the next day and then locked myself in the Gem Salon and burnt family papers till evening came. I went to dine at Hugues, all alone, and then went for a quiet stroll round the streets. I'll never forget that brisk, hazy April night, with the full moon shading a milky light on the apricot blossoms giving off their sweet mild fragrance. It was supposed to be my last night on earth. Now don't imagine I wanted to step out of this life on account of having lost my wealth: on the contrary, I had purposefully wasted it all because I had, for quite some time, decided to do away with a life I was tired of. The sights I had seen had only deepened my inborn melancholy, and the pleasures I had tasted had only given me a handsome share of disappointment and disgust. So, I had chosen my twenty-third birthday to leave the world of the living. I was to sneak out halfway through the party, never to return: no one would

ever find what had become of me, and I had taken every con-
ceivable step to keep the mystery of my disappearance sealed
forever. Till dawn, my mind conjured up sweet memories of
my boyhood that mellowed my heart, but were less than
could shake my determination, as my blood also contained
my ancestors' serenity in the face of death. And when I returned home, all calm and composed, I found a note that had
arrived in the late hours of the evening, and which summoned
me to court at noon that day: it was to inform me that my uncle Iorgu had been killed the day before.

'Though I came down in line as a nephew to him, I
had hardly ever met the man. The unbecoming marriage of
which he had been the offspring, followed by further family
discords, had drawn his father and himself away from relatives, with never a chance of reconciliation. His understand-
able hostility to them, all the bitterer as there was nothing he
could do in retaliation, was crudely dismissed with such utter
contempt as I, for one, can no longer share today. The man
had proved a man indeed! Instead of sitting comfortably on
whatever he had inherited from his parents, he went to lease
several estates, fish pools, customs points, salt mines; traded
extensively in lumber and wool; built an inn in Bucharest and
a wharf by the Danube. And fair lady Fortune was graceful
enough to handsomely reward his enterprise and earnest ap-
plication. The war, which he had served as the most reliable
army supplier, had made him the richest man in the country.
Even so, he couldn't help lending some destitute bloke a miserable gold piece or two for whatever the poor devil had to
put in pawn, as he would make little difference as to the
means when it came to gaining profit. It wasn't long since,
through faction and bribes, he had won the case in court

against the stout, headstrong yeomen for their share of the Toroipanu estate on the Neajlov River. He was going to make the measurements in the field, riding along the road that crossed the woods nearby, when he suddenly his carriage was surrounded by a handsome bunch of angry villagers. He stood up and drew his two pistols, but never managed to fire them: in a blink of an eye he was grabbed, snatched and pinned to the footboard of the carriage. What followed was a ruthless, savage execution.

'Now I was invited to attend the procedures of breaking the seals they had put on his bleak-looking house in Mântuleasa Street the night before. I had never imagined even the most parsimonious of men living in such utter poverty. I stood there, watching impassively as they searched the place, till the moment they opened a huge iron cabinet. At that point, my sudden amazement was not aroused by the treasure trove the shelves displayed, as much as at the sight of the same buckles and girdles I had, only the day before, given uncle Scarlat to put in pawn for me. Then my bills of exchange came up, all of them packed in a thick wad. Well, what more can I say? They combed and searched all over the place, scrutinized every written paper down to the last scrap, but there was no trace of an explicit testament—which made me, as his living next of kin, the lawful inheritor of his humongous fortune.

'The leeches who had benefited from my reckless generosity were the first to exult at this sudden, providential turn of the wheel: they thought the horn of plenty had opened once more for them. Bitter disappointment followed shortly, as it seemed as if my obscure uncle had, with his riches, bestowed on me some of his own character. It was not long before I closed down the house at the Red Fount and moved to Mântuleasa; I gave away my horses, coaches, hounds, everything; I dismissed all redundant servants, turned my back on my gleeful company, put an end to party sprees. And I lingered about not one day longer than what I needed to make every arrangement for a final goodbye.

'For I hadn't actually given up on my decision to disappear—I had only chosen to replace demise with departure. I realised I would, in time, have ended up a stranger to a place with nothing left to spur me along the way. Power and glory, you might say? Indeed, what could I possibly expect of a country where my father had declined a minister's position, and my great-grandfather had turned down the ultimate offer of the throne? Besides, I wouldn't have sacrificed my freedom for even the glorious star in the service of the emperor's guard. From now on, my own free will and fancy were to be my only guide ahead. Anything less than that would have made me unworthy of such good fortune as I had coming my way.

'And good fortune I did have—in abundance! Now, listen to this. It was the last night I was spending in Bucharest and, before going to bed, I went to take my passport out of an old chest of drawers—an ugly, mahogany Empire piece. As the drawer where I had put away my passport was crammed with what not, it stuck as I tried to pull it open. I took an hour to shake and snatch it open, and when it finally gave way, there's another hitch: the darn passport, which was on top of everything else, had slipped behind the drawers, which were designed so as not to slide completely off the chest. It was only my reverence for antiques that prevented me taking an axe and chopping the fiendish Empire to splinters. Instead, I settled for dislocating a panel at the back. There was my passport, at last—but not alone! A large yellow envelope lay beside it, patched with five black wax seals. It read: "My Will".

'At the sight of it, a chill shot up my spine like I had never felt before. I cast a wary glance around, though I knew I was all alone in the house. The October rain was tapping against the window shutters. I split the envelope open and held my breath as I read my uncle's last will: all of his movable and immovable property was to go to the Health Board of Trustees. I stood there perfectly perplexed, staring at the deadly giveaway which, had it fallen into hands other than mine, would have literally put my neck in the noose. There was little change in my state of mind as I was staring at the ashes the document had turned into, a few moments later. You may well say it was the wrong thing to do—I'll grant you that, but I've taken it upon myself to only account for my choice before the Almighty, who, as my aunt Smaranda would say, has special scales that give short measure for our sins. And I won't blush while confessing that those few lines made me freeze with fright, after I had so many times sneered in the face of death—because my very wealth and welfare were at stake this time, and God only knows there's nothing in the world I hold more sacred. Wealth is everything to me, it comes before honour, health, even life itself; and if that night, the memory of which still gives me the shivers, I had been pushed to something more hideous than destroy a scrap of paper—believe me, I wouldn't have faltered a moment, for I was not of feeble-minded stock!

To let go of such blessed abundance would have been a sin against my forebears. Without it my line of kin would

have missed, before forever sinking into oblivion, the fulfil-
ment of their true and natural calling—that of freely sailing
the seas, to the heart's content. I feel strongly that I gave a
nobler destination to all those riches than what my uncle had
intended in redemption for the nefarious ways by which he
had amassed them. For thirty long years I sailed the seas of
the world, some of which the sailors of my blood line had
never even heard of, and I often felt their pride swell in my
chest as I carried the arrow-stabbed swan of the house's stan-
dard throughout every voyage...'

He beckoned for the bill, as the waiter was pacing
around with a shade of impatience. The place was deserted.
We were the last to leave. We stepped outside into the clear,
crisp air.

'Yes, my friend,' he resumed after we had walked a
few steps, 'it's all about my possessions. Had it been otherwise, I'd never have come back here. The heavy riot of nine-
teen hundred and seven[111] made me think twice and, for fear
I might lose my estates, I finally decided to come over and
sell them away this spring—sell them at a loss, if bad came to
worse. But I was offered incredible prices, and guess by
whom? By the peasants themselves, mind you! It was on the
cards, it seems, for these people to line my pockets once

---

111 A peasants' revolt that broke up in March 1907 and quickly spread south to Wallachia.
Land ownership was the main cause for the commoners' discontent. The uprising was stifled
by the army, with casualties in the range of thousands.

more. Now really, you have no idea what decent, honourable characters these fellows can be; and what a difference between the pathetic humbletons I saw at the Red Fount back in my childhood days, stooping low like mongrels at the foot of the stairs before aunt Smaranda as if bedazzled by the radiance of her august majesty, and their proud offspring of today, standing upright, looking me in the eye, talking man to man. Then I wondered: where on earth did their community get all that money to pay down for almost ten thousand hectares of farmland? I was reckoning the same blessed wind would blow my sail to sell whatever buildings I owned in Bucharest, but I hit the wrong market here: it's been eight months now since a bunch of petty merchants have been putting me off over a shabby cot of a shop close to Bărăţia[112]. Not even when I registered my crude oil at the Stock Exchange in Amsterdam did I run through such groping negotiations—and my oil brings me more than three quarters of my income! The poor devils must have smelt my haste to leave.

'For all the trail of my fond memories, I've felt little more than a miserable exile since the very day I set foot again in this city—and it's how I always feel anywhere aground. Nothing can bring me to terms with the dry land except my devotion to flowers, which even my lust for the sea has been unable to subdue. Like my great-grandmother Păuna, who introduced new breeds into Wallachia and grew them across hectares in Pajera, I am hopelessly fond of flowers. It is indeed for my orchids, rather than myself—in fact, I am more of a guest to them—that I have purchased the

---

112 Bărăţia is the name of the oldest Roman Catholic church in Bucharest.

"Quinta Manuelina"[113] on the ocean coast, in a Lusitanian garden of Eden, an estate which used to host royal romances once. I rest my reveries between one voyage and the next in the fragrant moisture of spacious glasshouses, among bee-hives and lively spring waters. At the foot of those terraced gardens shall I board the last sailing ship to take me away on my last voyage, as soon as I feel the call for the last passage...

'Now why have they all closed? Can it be that late?' He looked up at the star-studded November sky: 'Indeed it's late. Orion, the golden hunter, is sinking westwards in fear of Scorpius scrambling up the eastern skies. But the dawn is a long way yet, so there's time enough for a few more rounds at my place.'

We left Modei Street when the lamp posts came alight again, with me somewhat bemused at the latest confessions.

For as long as he was to stay in Bucharest, ***[114] wanted to have the time all to himself, to kindle his sweet memories and move about freely, with no one to recognise him. So, he decided to change his look: he grew long hair, a beard and moustache, and donned an apparel of the most in-

---

113 Reference is made to the Quinta da Regaleira, an impressive estate and palace near Sintra, Portugal, built at the turn of the 20th c. in the romantic fashion. The place belongs today in the UNESCO World Heritage, after having passed from one owner to the next several times. This detail may have been speculated upon by Mateiu Caragiale to slip his fictitious character Pantazi in the line of the Quinta's owners.

114 The mark appears in the original with no further explanation—a hint of the author pretending to keep his character's real identity confidential.

conspicuous choice—such that, nearly a year later, he still had a shade of doubt about his own reflection in the mirror. Another, different man was looking at him from behind the glass, and it was not long before his new avatar acquired a new name: he was known as Master Pantazi round the pubs and bistros, which made him suspect he was taken for somebody of that name, a look-alike whom he still marvelled that, as it happened, he hadn't yet run into.

He had once shown me a photograph of his regular face: clean-shaven, with a clear forehead and trimmed short whiskers—the perfect gentleman in perfectly gentlemanlike attire on board a cruise ship. I had cast a dispassionate eye to the photo which showed a person perfectly strange to the one I had felt to be an age-old, long-lost friend, if not my alter-ego. I then realised that the incarnation of this feeling of mine, who was standing before me, was no more than a temporary disguise, soon to be forever discarded.

My apprehension that our friendship might lose some of its lustre in the wake of my disappointment proved to be entirely unfounded, as did my hope to return home early. In fact, it did not happen for a whole week. I moved in with Pantazi—I shall continue to call him by this name—who went to hide in his padded sanctuary and drew the curtains against the angry blizzard outside. Indeed he needed not go out, since his hostess had come to know all his quirks and twists and went about as if it was her life mission to pamper him to the best of his comfort. The beds were made ready for us at any time—I had been given my own in the salon. The table was laid, the candelabra lit through day or night, the fire was roaring in the stoves. In torpid idleness, the confession of his life as a citizen of the universe trickled freely into an accomplished design. And so I came to realise the only possible reason for that deep melancholy in him, so utterly disconcerting to me: if anything, the man had been overly gratified with a blissful life.

Nothing could be sweeter than those halcyon days for all the storm outside, and even when it had ceased its rage we were both reluctant to break the bliss of carefree repose. Until one morning—we knew the time of day by the hot chocolate that had been served to us—when the hostess rushed in, sour and surly and red in the face, to inform Pantazi a gentleman was asking about him, a foul-mouthed gentleman and a dog with him; utterly rude to her he was... Pantazi asked me to see who it was, while he and the Frenchwoman drew the curtains away and put out the candles.

As the daylight flooded in Pirgu followed, dragging behind a tiny pug, all shrivelled with cold and wrapped in a fitting caparison. We learned that Paşadia, who had returned only the day before, had been searching the pubs and bistros for us all night and finally asked him, Pirgu, to find us, with an invitation for lunch. Pantazi accepted without a blink. I asked Gore about his four-legged companion while the latter was busy snarling and barking at Pantazi.

'He belongs to Haralambescu,' he explained; 'Tinculina Caiduri has a virgin bitch in heat, a Carlin too, so I'm providing. See, I'm into dog pandering now.'

This time, the nights that followed in Paşadia's company had a quiet and dignified quality about them. Pirgu had become a sparse and transient presence, and when he did attend, he pestered us with politics. The Liberals were packing up, he said, and the Conservatives, the blueblood, would come to power by New Year's Eve into 1911, only three weeks away; Take[115] was at the end of his rope, he said. And he put on those lofty airs, in anticipation of the high office he claimed would be assigned to him by the coming government.

Though I knew him to be insatiably greedy, capable even to stoop for a farthing, I didn't take long to understand that the end of his pursuit was by no means a regular income; and I would never have suspected what he was after, had he not told me himself about it on Christmas Eve, while on a drinking spree—the 'adult measure', he called it.

Marriage had long been his idea of climbing the ladder of affluence and success, but he had been spurned every time he proposed, and even when the girl happened to like him, he couldn't go past the parents' rebuff. This ostracism, he said, could have no other cause than that he didn't display a 'solid career'—for otherwise, what was it he might miss to make a woman into a happy wife? Handsome, young, 'well-behaved', cultivated and all that? On the other hand, there would be little resistance if a minister spoke in favour of his dear principal private secretary, a most promising, earnest

---

115 Take (Tache) Ionescu was an outstanding Romanian politician, journalist, lawyer and diplomat. He is generally viewed as embodying the rise of middle-class politics in the early-20th-century Kingdom of Romania. He switched from radical liberalism to conservative politics and eventually founded his own Conservative-Democratic Party in 1891. Take Ionescu is assigned an important contribution to the foundation of Greater Romania in the wake of World War 1.

young man whom he, the minister, were ready to assist in marriage. And once appointed into the office the road would be open for him, a bigwig, heavyweight, with loads of gravy, a sumptuous mansion in Bucharest, a vineyard in bearing at the Valley of the Lambs[116], some handsome estate some place, plus one single brother in law with one single lung to breathe what little was left of his life. And he sang: 'And lo, he has aplenty, and lo, he has aplenty!' I broke in with a question: had he given the slightest thought to the two parapherna that hung in the wake of marriage: offspring and cuckolding?

'Don't you worry about it none,' he said in a calm, reassuring tone, 'the damsel has tasted of the both before. Such parapherna are small fry, they don't fall in the stakes here.'

Now that drove me into the corner. I asked him who was going to intercede for him, after all—and, although no one was around to listen in, he secretly whispered the answer into my ear: 'Paşa.'

'Think he can do it?'

'Do it?! You wouldn't believe what the old goat's carrying in his pants, only let him put it on the scales and you'll see hell's a-poppin'!'

'But then, why would he be standing back?' I asked in an attempt to shake more out of him.

---

116 Valea Mieilor (Valley of the Lambs): a vinicultural area in Prahova County, not very far from Bucharest.

Two short whistles and two fingers wiggling against his temple was all I could get for an answer. Then Gorică left, pacing backwards, and stopped in the doorway to show me the sign of Harpocrates[117].

One evening between Christmas and New Year's Eve I was strolling down Victoria Road as it was uncommonly lively, bustling with people. Newspaper boys pulled open the strings round the stacks as they ran and shouted their hearts out: 'Government resigns! Government steps down!' While walking past the Palace gardens I heard my name called out from under the raised hood of a hackney coach. It was Pirgu.

'Hey doc,' he said, 'go find Paşadia and tell him to clear his hands of whatever he's got on them and rush to put down his bollocks for my case—tonight—now—no delay!'

I asked, why didn't he do it himself?

'No time,' he explained, 'I'm busy with Mişu's funeral, I must lend a hand to the disconsolate widow—what are friends for, after all? I'm on my way now from the Jewish Cemetery to the news room. Ha! There's a big fuss over the houses: old Faibiş Nachmansohn is flat broke, he built them on a site he'd bought in his late dame's name, Mişu's mother; he lay down everything to build them, to the last chip. Now he lost it all: Mişu has left them to Raşelica, legal papers and all—she's nobody's fool, is she? She'd made Penchas, her ex, do the same for her... You should see her in mourning garb—dazzling, absolutely dazzling! A devil of a woman, I tell you: Mişu was breathing his last in the next room while

---

117 The god of silence in Greek mythology, represented as a child sucking his finger.

the two of us... *tu comprends?*[118] Clinging like a leech she was—but she took off her hat to me, too. Now you hurry up and get the old goat before he's out for the night—you won't let me down, will you!'

He swore at the cabbie and ordered him to move on. As the carriage started on its way, he poked his head out once more and added: 'Come to the cemetery after tomorrow, I'll be giving a speech.'

*

„Profundum est cor super omnia—et homo est—et quis cognoscet eum?"

(Jer. 17:9)[119]

A quarter of an hour later I was ringing at Paşadia's door, armed with the assurance of one who pleads in another's behalf. I knew he was in as soon as I had seen, farther down the yard, the flickering lanterns of a brougham in waiting.

This time I was not, as usual, ushered straightaway into his study: the elderly butler who let me in relieved me of my coat and hat and then asked me to abide. The flames

---

118 French for: Do you understand?

119 From Latin: The heart is deceitful above all things, and desperately wicked: who can know it? (Jeremiah 17:9, King James Version)

dancing playfully round the logs in the generous fireplace gave all the light there was in the anteroom, casting eerie shadows that called to life the old canvases on the walls, like windows opening on days of yore, unfurling frightful scenes of martyrdom and dire scourge. Centurions in the service of Domitianus or Decius[120], leaning against their spears, alongside fierce horsemen of the desert riding their fiery stallions, while gleefully gloating over the excruciating agony of crucified maidens or juveniles pierced by arrows, all under a somber canopy of grey clouds swirling above stray livid leafage. I took my time looking at those gloomy frames that lined Paşadia's sanctuary and the lot of them returned a sense of the deep torment inside him.

Suddenly the lights went on, and the mirrors gave back a thousand candelabra. The butler turned up shortly to invite me upstairs.

It was the first time I was climbing up those stairs sentinelled by Baroque sphinxes; then I was led through a suite of rooms that were even more packed with valuable artefacts, which made me feel I had entered a museum rather than a private home. A surprising sight stopped me short in the doorway of the last chamber.

Paşadia in tailcoat, complete with blue ribbon and decorations, was certainly not headed for the brothel or the gambling house that evening. Moreover, his very appearance was a dramatic difference from what I knew him to be: he looked rejuvenated, with none of the usual signs of fatigue in

---

120 Domitianus (81-96 A.D.), and Decius (249-251 A.D.), Roman emperors of notorious cruelty.

his mien or on his face, and his voice bore a crisp, metallic quality. I found it hard to give him credit as he contended he hadn't felt so bored in a long, long time.

His blessed privacy had been shattered, he said, by a most unexpected couple of visitors: a high official from Austria and his wife, who had stopped in Bucharest for three days on their way to Egypt. Directly upon arrival, the fellow inquired after his old-time schoolmate Paşadia, never to let him loose since the moment they met. Paşadia even had to chaperon the lady to The Ant[121] and assist her while purchasing a fair collection of hand-made Romanian blouses. On top of all, they had insisted on his attending the formal dinner offered by the Austrian mission in their honour that evening. A pestering headache, in all.

I made a heartfelt silent wish that such pestering headaches might cross his path more often. Knowing he would plunge for a few hours into the kind of life he had been truly born to live, it occurred to me he might feel some deep stir within, perhaps a shade of tardy regret at having turned his back on it. The furtive glance I cast in his direction met the same impassive, impenetrable figure which, to my mind, must have been hiding the mute agony of an old noble breed.

I told him I would have felt flattered and impressed in his place: those people had been more than nice to him, and their behaviour was perfect credentials for their genuine affection.

---

121 Furnica (The Ant), a popular ladies' shop dating back in early 20th c. Bucharest.

'You are mistaken,' he said; 'it is nothing but pure interest: this journey they are making is but a disguise for an important political mission. The Balkans have been smouldering with unrest for three years now, and the gears are grinding across chancelleries. They've even remembered me, of all people... No—believe me, it's all bad all the way, no place in sight for doing something good, or at least nice.'

Since the conversation had touched upon amity, I seized the opportunity to let him into the reason for my visit. At that, he gave a wry smile.

'I may well be crazy, like they say, but not all that crazy as to hoist Pirgu to the top of the ladder!'

And yet, I had lately heard him more than once pledging his full support to his inseparable companion, till the latter was deprived of all fear of failure.

'Not only have I not pressed for his appointment in some high office,' he added, 'but I have taken certain precautions to avoid it. This isn't the first time I'm going behind his back; If I hadn't—what do you think?—the crooked rascal would have long been on his way up by now, from chief of cabinet to prefect to secretary general to Parliament membership; and he would have wriggled his way into a profitable marriage too, had it not been for me to turn the tables. It certainly is the most righteous and honest thing I've done in all my life; it would have been against all morals to do otherwise. Apart from that, if I were to let him rise I'd lose him, and I can't afford to miss his services.

'A lamentable case, if I may say so. But for the sake of getting my share of the game with ease while staying clear of the deepermost squalor of vice, I have to abide the company of this ghoul, feed him and breathe the fetid stench of his ways. But what is it that makes *you* sail in the wake of such a disgusting specimen? Your sense of humour, I believe, is not the kind that feeds on his gross lewdness. I have long wanted to warn you to beware of him: he is capable of all evil, and doesn't belong in the lot whom the benefit of cowardice would hold back from murder—in fact, he's got more than one on his hands. Be careful, he is loaded with rancour against you, but he can't as yet go any further than besmirch you with vile gossip. The other night, he and Poponel were having a high time burning you in effigy, as it were—oh yes, the same Poponel to whose defence you are forever standing up as foolishly naïve as you've been tonight to intercede with me on Pirgu's behalf.

'In fact, I am annoyed to observe your reprehensible inclination towards whatever bears the mark of corruption, towards the garbage and the wreckage of this world, and should you tell me it's only for the purpose of studying and sampling a little of everything, I still would find you no excuse—for you would then be paying a terribly high price for a terribly vile merchandise.

'I tell you, his bohemian world is truly monstrous—murderous even, often beyond the metaphorical protection of the word. And as I care for your person more than your friendship, I have no fear my words might hurt your vanity. Here I am, venturing my angry assault against the deplorable life style you have adopted of late, but I will fain swallow my tongue if you can convince me you are at peace with your conscience and in perfect contentment, and that after those moments of self-oblivion you don't feel the pangs of dignity abused.'

Without waiting for my answer to that, he continued:

'I told you the story of the precarious, painful life I lived for quite a long time—which, you must admit, would give me every reason to match my status to that of a Talmudic mamzer[122]. And you know how, years and years—*grande mortalis aevi spatium*[123]—I struggled in vain for vainglorious values. Well, believe it or not, I feel nostalgic for those times, for all the tension and the turmoil that exhilarated me then. But when the persecution stopped and I suddenly found myself in a position I had long given up hope to reach, I was seized with bitterness.

'Far from a romantic nature, my self-regard received a heavy blow however, as I realised that thirty long years of sacrifice, earnest study and arduous work had not been enough to achieve what I readily obtained after a few nights beside the influential wife of a council chairman. It didn't take me long to conclude that my spectacular success was but a treacherous trap that Fortune had laid before me in token of her unfathomable sense of irony. The prayer of my heart's desire was fully answered: all the power, money and distinctions I had long craved for were finally there, within my reach. And yet, far from bringing me the least satisfaction,

---

122 In Jewish religious law, a mamzer is the offspring of an incestuous or an adulterous union. In Jewish and Yiddish, mamzer has also acquired a colloquial connotation defining a worldly-wise person.

123 From Latin: a lengthy span in a mortal's lifetime (Tacitus, Agricola).

the whole thing was a pain in the neck, I took bitter offence at flattering compliments, nor could I rejoice in revenge. I was left with two alternatives: either hold fast to the newly acquired position, at the cost of deluding myself into a fraudulent—and permanent—moral failure, or else sound the retreat. I owed myself the elegance of choosing the latter. So, in the face of whatever hopeless and pointless life was left for me to live, I decided it was no more use trying to fight the demon which, since early youth, has never failed to nudge me into temptation at nightfall.

'They who knew me were wondering why I didn't consider leaving the country. You will remember the story about the Italian who came to Paris in the days of Louis XIV, was presently taken to the Bastille and left in oblivion there for thirty-five long years before he was eventually tried and found perfectly innocent during the early days of the Regency[124], and how the poor soul dejectedly refused his freedom and asked to be left to the end in confinement. It was very much my case—to the point that I might be his reincarnation, I'd think. What was there left for me in the world after all? Nothing to move me, nothing to please me, absolutely nothing; and if I still kindle such weary passions as study, the arts, reading and writing, it's only to kill time. Truth to tell, and leaving metaphor aside, I might say I hardly feel alive: my soul has been dozing the years away before the gates of the abode of Death, waiting for the call. Now the reward for such enduring patience is near: a fathomless fall into infinite forgetfulness.'

---

124 The French Regency of Philippe, Duc d'Orléans (1715-1723).

'Oh no,' I exclaimed, 'not forgetfulness, of all things! All the work you've been so masterly adding up to for thirty years now will be an accomplished plea for your immortality.'

'Out of the question! My work will be gone with me. As soon as I've closed my eyes to this world, a faithful hand shall destroy everything that stays written here. As you will have seen, the closets in my study are walled in and hidden behind heavy drapery, so as one shouldn't easily notice they have no bottom and open down into a tunnel. So before they come to seal them up, let alone open them later, the faithful hand will have done its duty.'

His last words made me wince, for I knew him for a man who would always put his heart where his mouth was. So, a pile of works worthy of reverence across the centuries were doomed to be forever lost to the world—pages that easily matched the brilliance of Cardinal de Retz[125], Saint-Simon[126], or Tacitus[127] himself. My heart sank at the thought, overcome by rending grief.

---

125 Jean François Paul de Gondi, Cardinal de Retz (1613-1679), was a French churchman, politician and writer. His Memoirs of Cardinal de Retz were written in a worldly, brisk, sometimes frivolous style.

126 Louis de Rouvroy, Duke de Saint-Simon (1675-1755), was a French soldier and writer. His Mémoires, describing life at King Louis XIV's court, are an important historic document of his time.

127 Publius (or Gaius) Cornelius Tacitus (AD 56 – AD 117) was a senator of Rome and a historian of the Roman Empire. His work features a bold, sharp wit, and a concise, sometimes unconventional style.

'As I had been raised away from my native land from early childhood,' he resumed his confession, 'it was some time before I learnt I was living on the doorstep of the Orient, where public morals are upside down and nothing is taken seriously. With such headstrong determination as didn't pay credit to my intelligence, but which I do not regret, for I wouldn't do otherwise if I were to start again, I refused to adapt and merge with their ways, although I had learnt that *si Romae vivis, romano vivite more*[128]. No wonder that I was treated like a stranger and everybody gave me the cold shoulder. Against my better feelings, I had to engage in a confrontation that came in dissonance with my true nature. When their derision failed to get the better of me—for my backlash was a lot more vicious—they wove a conspiracy of silence round whatever I had started to publish. Then I decided that the only adequate way to retaliate was to leave behind nothing that would benefit or please anyone. Since I am not prone to cheap vanities, I welcomed their conspiracy and joined in myself. "Ungrateful fatherland, thou shalt not even have my bones" is what Scipio Africanus[129] ordered for his epitaph. Well, I am letting them have my bones, but not the fruit of my thoughts, the vintage crop of my meditations— not that, ever!

---

128 From Latin: If you live in Rome, you should follow the way of the Romans.

129 Publius Cornelius Scipio (235-183 BC), aka Scipio Africanus and Scipio the Elder, was a general in the Second Punic War and statesman of the Roman Republic. He led the victorious campaign against Hannibal at Zama, a feat that ranges him with the finest commanders in military history. His popularity in Rome brought him political hostility, against which he retaliated by refusing to be buried in Rome and ordering the famous epitaph: Ingrata patria, ne ossa quidem habebis.

He consulted his watch with what seemed to be a shade of disquiet. I stood up and prepared to leave.

'Stay awhile,' he said, 'we'll go together; you'll escort me to the place.' In a muffled tone, he added: 'It's safer.'

I walked back through the suite of salons that provided a shrine for the lingering gallant age, swinging between Olympian heavy colours and idyllic mush in ornamental flower frame. In a dark corner of the most richly ornate of those rooms my attention was swept by a gloomy portrait that came into sharp contrast with all the delicate wonders that crammed the place: a man of a totally different stock from the gents and the ladies that stared at one-another with sly or languid smiles from the other frames. The man's resemblance to Paşadia was incredibly close, you might have said his duplicate, only somewhat younger and dressed up in the ugly century-old boyars' attire.

'My great-grandfather,' Paşadia explained. 'The only one of the family who gained my sympathy; the only one whose portrait I spared from the fire. He was a Bergami. His handsome haughty bearing, crowned by a woman's fascination for those who have taken a human life, swept him from behind Princess Ralu's chariot into her bed. He was rewarded with Măgura estate and the provost marshal's mace. As you can see, what's bred in the bone won't go out of the flesh; our frames of mind, too, bear much resemblance—to think of how, in the heyday of youth, he freely let them poison him.

'This portrait is among the few things I own here, most of them just rented.'

117

Still talking, we walked slowly down the stairs. Iancu Mitan, the faithful butler and another two valets stood in attendance there. Still other servants peeped their heads from behind the doors in compelling curiosity. The carriage made a brisk start and soon we were in Vienna Street.

'If you meet Pirgu,' he advised me before parting, 'tell him I have proceeded to the best of my judgment and that tonight I am leaving... for the mountains.'

Twilight of the Gallants

„Vous pénétrerez dans les familles, nous

peindrons des intérieurs domestiques, nous

ferons du drame bourgeois[130], des grandes et

des petites bretêches."[131]

Monselet[132]

As spring drew near, such outings became more frequent and lasted longer. Every time, as soon as he returned,
Paşadia would invite us to dinner. He and Pantazi were getting closer with each passing day, and as I suspected there

---

130 Bourgeois drama refers to serious drama about people of apparently unheroic status, as
opposed to the tragic protagonists of drama in Aristotelian terms. Bourgeois drama dates
back to the 18th century and continues to be highly significant in our days.

131 From French: You will be introduced to private families, we shall depict domestic inte-
riors, we shall do bourgeois drama and raise fortifications large and small.

132 Charles Montselet (1825-1888) was a French journalist, novelist, poet and playwright.
Also known as the "Prince of Parisian gourmets", he wrote the Almanach des gourmands
and the Cuisine Poétique.

might be matters they would rather discuss in private, I decided I might as well say good bye right after coffee, like Pirgu did, and leave them alone for a few hours.

Before we reached the gate, I never failed to inquire Pirgu about his destination, so that I might declare the opposite direction. Once, however, he was the first to ask me where I was headed, and I ventured the Academy.

'I had no idea they opened again,' he said, 'I'm surprised I'm the last to learn. But they'll bungle it again, you'll see. Billiards is out of fashion these days; only the hazelnut sellers[133] are still playing "three-cushion" or "snooker"—pity though, they were nice games, really.'

As he insisted on coming along, I had to explain it was not about the Billiards Academy, but the Romanian Academy. He inquired about my business there and was genuinely disappointed to hear that I was going there to read. He went on to berate me.

'Aren't you ever going to grow up, mate? Cram all that bookish stuff into your brains and you'll end up a raving maniac like Paşadia. What's it to you if you get to know who midwived Mohammed or what was the name of the first chap to pick out the Cross on Epiphany[134]? It's nothing, I tell you:

---

133 Hazelnut seller was a derisive term for a Greek.

134 Epiphany, or Theophany, is a Christian feast day (January 6) celebrating the revelation of God the Son in the person of Jesus Christ. The Orthodox Churches perform the Great Blessing of Waters on Theophany. Following the Divine Liturgy, the clergy and people go in a Crucession (a procession with the cross) to the nearest body of water (ideally, it should be a body of "living water"). At the end of the ceremony the priest will bless the waters by

you'll only get withered before your time on it. The true knowledge is elsewhere: it's getting to know the ways of the world you're moving in, something you're a perfect stranger to, and you won't get any of it in those books of yours.

'Before you arrived today, I almost burst out laughing when I heard you're working on a novel about Bucharest morals and manners. Really mate, what the deuce do you know about Bucharest manners? Chinese rather, for you're no closer than a Chink to the matter. How on earth will you get to learn anything about morals and manners as long as you aren't acquainted with the people around? Or maybe you're only just going to write about us: Paşa, me, Panta... do I know anyone else you know?—ah, yes, good old friend Poponel! Now, if you went about visiting places and families, rubbing elbows with the neighbourhood, that would make a difference: you'd be surprised at the variety of subjects you'd find, and all the queer birds you'd come across! Well, I just happen to know such a place...'

I was prompt to oblige:

'The Arnoteanus', the true-blood Arnoteanus'.'

His gesture was meant to cancel all doubt; then he added, with a wink and a smile:

'The gambling runs through the night and we get our share, we'll provide the harlots of course; they'll be staking

---

casting a cross into the water and volunteers will swim to recover it. The first to get to the cross swims back and returns it to the priest, who then delivers a special blessing to the swimmer and his house.

their purses and we, the unmercenary healers, will stand by kiebitzing.'

While serving him the same flat promise that so many times before had dodged his pestering persistence to drag me to that house of ill repute, I had no idea I would be the one to make his dream come true, no later than the next time Paşadia invited us to dinner.

Rather tired of scholarly pedantries lately, I felt a compulsory need for exhilaration. And indeed that day, the cascade of antics and drolleries that Gorică performed from noon till late evening was enough compensation for every reason he had given me to detest him. He was wild with hysterical gaiety, and Paşadia all but turned him out at some point. I had never seen him bathing in such farcical histrionics and frantic exuberance, a long way from his usual disposition, and it was not before the end of the day that he disclosed the cause: his old man had died.

He sneered off the condolences that Pantazi and myself hasted to extend and told us to cut the trivia.

'I'd be happier with you comforting me for the Almighty taking such a long time to shake the miserable bastard off my back,' he added.

Had the honourable Sumbasacu Pirgu bit the dust some ten or twelve years ago, and left the twenty thousand lei due to each of his eight children, the surviving stock out of seventeen—would then Gore have ended up nursing a bunch of decrepit dodderers? Oh, what a man he would have made! The most brilliant barrister, second to none round the Romanian courts of law! He would have stood in defence of

Paşadia charged with indecent assault, and pleaded not guilty on account of the defendant's erectile dysfunction. Yes, a lawyer—and a University professor! He would have wasted some time on literature too, lashing at the easy virtues of the day and writing cheesy historical drama—and he went on to improvise lengthy, tedious pieces of dialogue between characters from different ages, act out fragments from this or that leading part, dangling legs and swinging arms about, snorting or bellowing through the lines... But would that be all? Oh no! An expansive champion of the ultimate claims of democracy, he would have pleaded in Parliament for putting the peasants in possession of their own land and for the public vote. At that, there and then, he engaged in a fluent speech, no less pathetic and vain and hollow than what you could usually hear under the dome on top of Metropolitanate Hill[135]... Moreover, his distinguished appearance would have been an asset for the diplomatic career, even if he lacked a quirky twist like that of Poponel—but then again, even that could have been arranged, with Paşadia at hand... On the other hand, his sweet dream had always been a patriarchal country life: to handle the plow in good conscience, to till his own land...

'All nice and fine,' I said, 'but what are you actually going to go for, now that you've finally stepped into this handsome inheritance?'

---

135 The old seat of the Chamber of Deputies of Romania (until 1997), close to the Romanian Patriarchal Cathedral and the Patriarchal Palace.

'Well, my dear sir,' he said, 'I'm going to be a big fish at the Stone Cross[136], with my own matron lady and a train of dollies to cuddle, and my private personal pimp to blow the trumpet. And I'll sit in for church guardian too—and later, when old age gets the better of me, I'll go to the monastery, cross my heart I will!...'

And he introduced himself as pious monk Gherasim, Ghideon or Gherontie, in devoted service of the Lord, chief psalm singer at Darvari Hermitage near Icoanei Park, thoughtlessly slipping in a "call" or a "check"[137] when his turn came to read his part. And, as a token of his ecclesiastic vocation, he went on to mumble and snuffle, in mock-clerical tones, a profane tangle of holy chants and mundane songs: *Sweet Spring* and *From Cherry-tree to Cherry-tree*, *Christ is Resurrected* and *Ma parole d'honneur mon cher*, or *Praise the Lord* and *I haram bam ba*. Pantazi laughed himself to tears, while Paşadia sat back in helpless resignation. Then Gore suddenly dropped silent, raised his right hand with the index finger pointing to his ear and stood still, as if petrified. Pantazi asked him what.

'What, can't you hear?' he said. 'Listen: *The trumpet sounds in bold accord, the proud tricolour pounds windward...*' Then he started yelling in mock-despair: *'Here's my musket, let it rattle, all I want is die in battle, not in slavery like a minion, give me, give me now my stallion!'* He

136 Crucea de Piatră (the Stone Cross) was a notorious brothel in Bucharest till after World War II.

137 Actions declared during a poker game wager: call, match the current bet; check, pass the action to the next player.

mounted his chair and made to charge, but tripped against the carpet edge and fell flat over an ice bucket that failed to hurt him as, back on his feet in an instant, he went to glide across the floor to show us how he would be dancing the great *hora*[138] to unite all Romanians, across the Carpathians, between the Tisa and the Dniester. And he yelled and whined and mimed, all contortions and grimaces: '*With a hey, and a ho, and a flower at the straw, up you go, round you go, ho, ho, ho, ho!*'

Then he vanished without a word and returned shortly, his pants down, his shirt hanging loose round his thighs. He looked glum and disconsolate. He was living the most providential day of his life, he said, with a blissful bright future beaming on him—alas, unlike on Paşadia—and on such a day we still denied to humour him and join him on a visit to the Arnoteanus', the true-blood Arnoteanus. And why ever not, for Pete's sake? Did we not know there was no more enjoyable place for an easygoing gamble at Cat and Mouse, or Baccarat Chemin de Fer, or Poker? What better place for that, hey? Or a light wine and soda, a cognac, a Turkish coffee, where could you find the best of that? At the Arnoteanus' of course! Or a sweet lass to cuddle to your heart's desire, hey? Where did you find that? Always at the Arnoteanus', the true-blood Arnoteanus, the only noble seed left, blessed with every Christian virtue. Admittedly, Maiorică was a contemptible idiot—but madam Elvira, what a perfect matron! And the girls, what a pair of pussycats—or better, outright *stallionesses*! Ha! If we refused him, it was only to hurt him, to martyrise him—what a shame, to treat a

---

138 Hora is a round dance in Romanian folklore.

confrere like that!... He sagged in utter misery, raised the lap of his shirt to cover his face and burst into bitter sobs and tears.

Not that he lacked a shade of candour, but even so, Gore deserved none of our sympathy, as he was the only one to blame for being unable to fulfil his miserable ambition. Indeed, since he knew we would fain walk in his steps without question, every night he found us in Paşadia's company, then what easier thing for him but to take us there without asking our consent and keeping the destination to himself? On the other hand, if the thought had crossed his mind— which was most likely, in fact—, he might have had some reason for restraint to act on it. With our stubborn reluctance so far to approach that abode of frivolous entertainment, he simply could not believe his ears as he heard me dropping a casual 'Why don't we call at the honourable Arnoteanus' tonight?', followed suit by Pantazi's 'Why not indeed?,' and finally, by Paşadia's noncommittal assent. Stricken with almost unbearable joy, it was a miracle Pirgu didn't lose whatever was left of his mind at that moment: he sunk to the floor and rolled over, head over heels, squealing and yelling and whining, and we had a hard time dissuading his intention of leading us there while mounted on one of the brougham's horses.

I cannot be blamed for my total ignorance of the name of the street that ran in front of the Arnoteanus' front gate, as for a whole month of regular attendance I went in and out of their fenceless back yard, which gave on to the right-hand embankment of the Dâmboviţa[139], upstream from

---

139 Dâmboviţa, pronounced ['dəmbovitsa], is the river which crosses Bucharest.

Mihai Vodă[140]. It was the more convenient access, since there was no one around to see me sneak in.

Memories of my first visit are quite disagreeable. For a full hour I was confronted with my own conscience and deplored my disgraceful decline. Good God, the company I had to partake that night, and the hands I had to shake! It was not long since Paşadia's bitter reproof, which kept ringing in my ears with ruthless persistence. A perfectly lamentable evening, had it been only for the fathomless ennui. Pirgu was no longer being funny, he was now bossing around making arrangements for the gambling tables, having the players toss for the best seats. He quickly distributed Paşadia for a poker party and Pantazi for chemin-de-fer, each with two women standing on either side. The sudden silence that preceded the opening hand gave away a rustle of stifled cackling, moaning, and soft whispers.

At some point I felt it was time for me to take a French leave, with a mind to leave behind what I thought was the first and last visit to that place. In the doorway, the minute I thought I was saved, I ran into "Mama's Dearest", which is what they used to call madam Masinca Drîngeanu, as she herself addressed everybody else.

'I see,' she said, 'so you're sneaking out, shying away from seeing me back home. You don't love me any more...'

---

140 Mihai Vodă is the name given to an old church in central Bucharest and one of the bridges nearby across the Dâmboviţa. The name was given after Voivode Michael the Brave (1593-1601), the first ruler who managed to unite the three Romanian provinces (Wallachia, Moldova and Transylvania) for a short time.

And she extended her gloved hand, palm upwards, so I could put a kiss in the free gap left above the wrist.

'My dear lady,' I interrupted her, 'I will fain stand rebuked before all and every accusation in the world, save that!'

Indeed there was more than flimsy flattery to my compliment, for the woman had an appeal one could not easily ignore. Not only had her beauty managed to delude her age, like she herself had deluded two lawfully wedded husbands besides a long trail of other occasional lovers, but there was a certain magic in her bearing, which she wielded in such a way as you could simply not escape it. I presently forgot about my decision to leave while watching the scene of an unusually warm welcome, even among Romanians, as the lady of the house and both of her daughters rushed to embrace and kiss the newcomer in a flurry of enthusiasm, with vying eagerness to expose their affection. As she had just returned from Nice, questions rained in about how she had fared there, with no breath left for an answer. To cut their overwhelming invitations for a treat, "Mama's Dearest" finally decided on a cup of coffee and a Cointreau to go with it. She declined to enter fourth hand in a Cat and Mouse game and turned to me. We sat down at a small table in front of a large mirror that reflected every move in the next-door parlour, where the gambling was running.

She insisted to know why I had been in such a hurry to leave—some rendezvous, perhaps? I made no secret of the real reason, and she admitted she was partly sharing my distaste; she was not herself particularly partial to the like of Frosa Bojogescu or Gore Pirgu. But what did I expect? It was an inevitable mark of any gambling place, after all. On the other hand, what else could matter less when compared to the exclusive privilege of the Arnoteanus' company?

Not Maiorică, she certainly didn't mean him: Maiorică was such a perfect idiot! And yet, he was consistent with himself in some ways—a quality one could not possibly fail to appreciate, at least. Poor as a church mouse, head over heels in debt, rejected by relatives who had long turned their back on him, avoided by the rank and fashion, slandered and scoffed by most, he remained unruffled, forever exhibiting the same haughty airs and pathetic hot-tempered outbursts. Utterly indifferent to whatever was not of direct concern to his person, he lacked the faintest feeling for his wife and daughters: he wouldn't have flinched to see them die before his eyes, nay, he would have fain worn a pair of leather gloves made from their skin. His progeny, worthy of their father, would in turn have carried purses made from his raw-hide, which needed little tanning to make into leather. His wife was the only one left to love and eagerly look after him to the brink of sacrifice, very much like a bondmaid; she would tend his every need and want, easily crossing the commonly accepted boundary of repulsion, though she knew her "baby major"[141], as she used to call him, to be attending other women who were not exactly high-class, and from whom he returned penniless and sometimes ruffled, scratched or bruised. It had probably happened that very day, as he re-frained from gambling, smiled wryly and rubbed an eye sur-mounted by a respectable bump. I watched his pathetic flimsy figure in the slanted mirror above my head as he was

---

141 Maiorică is a diminutive for maior (Romanian for the military rank of major).

proudly clicking his heels around, raising on his toes here and there to peep over a kibitzer's shoulder. I tried in vain to find the least similarity between that elderly gypsy's wrinkled skull and the curly-haired officer gazing from a weathered photograph on a small table nearby, slender and graceful as he used to be at the time when Coriolan the barber had recorded him in his ledger as 'piccolo ma simpatico'[142]. Definitely, his callousness was of no more service to him than his plump consort's throbbing hormones were to her. With features still behind her age, she was cheerfully walking her ample, sallow, flaccid meat loaf among the guests, swinging her limp breasts and copious hips; she was all laughs and jests, with a word and a smile for everyone. And yet, I suspected her exuberance was a mask to conceal some deep-rooted sorrow, the source of which I presently surmised to be her husband's infidelity and her daughters' depravity. But Masinca was prompt to clear my confusion: as it happened, Elvira had been no stranger to the girls' decline; as for the infidelity part, with all due respect, she didn't fall behind Maiorică, was regularly en carte[143] with him, if not a few steps ahead. So the reason for her discontent had to be sought elsewhere. The Arnoteanus might sometimes miss their daily bread, but they certainly didn't let one single day go by without a brawl; and if only they had kept it to the vocal part—not a chance, ever! The girls would always come to fierce grips, grappling each-other's hair, scratching and biting and hurling whatever they could lay hands on, and tearing each-other's clothes; finally, they would both come down upon their mother and

---

142 Italian for slender but nice.

143 En carte (French): level with, on equal terms with sb.

beat the living daylights out of her. Her desperate screams brought the neighbours or passers-by to the rescue. And Maiorică? Well, Maiorică—"the billy goat", as they nick-named him—kept within safe distance, and only when he saw that push came to shove did he rush outside and, in his snuffling voice, he called out for the "mmm-police". He had learnt his lesson as, on a May 10th[144], when he had put on his military outfit to attend the parade, he got decorated from head to foot with a splash of marinated sauce. For a whole year, while she had let part of her house to the Arnoteanus—who hardly ever paid their rent, in fact—, Masinca had no use going to the theatre, and she often found it hard to decide whether she should laugh or cry at their scenes.

Indeed, the girls made a terrible combination, calam-ity incarnate! Mima, the elder, in particular, who was only fifteen when she first kindled the talk of the town as she had infatuated two young nincompoops at Galați, where her fa-ther was then quartered with the troops. She had asked one of the lads, the only child of a well-off family, to steal some jewellery from his mother. The other one, who had a job as a cashier with a wholesaler, was duped into immoderate ex-penses, to the foreseeable effect of foolishly slipping his fin-gers in the till. Predictably enough, it was not long before the culprits were discovered. Overwhelmed with disgrace, the well-off progeny blasted his brains out, while the shop boy went behind the bars for a year. A further victim in the wake of the episode was poor Maiorică, whose frail military career was thus finally and permanently disrupted. On the other hand, the true moral offender was left unscathed, even proud

144 May 10th used to be Romania's National Day.

of her nefarious feat as it ensured most of her success with the opposite sex. And yet, she never managed—or never knew how—to capitalize on that success beyond unlimited freedom to pathetic depravity. In vain had Masinca tried to teach her the art of seduction: Mima was no game for the school of the coy shepherdess who throws the apple of temptation and then runs in hide behind the willow tree—the age-old, though forever young, school of coquetry. The secret chemistry induced by the murderously slowly falling veils, one by one to the last but one, the subtle ritual of teasing and freezing, the oldest tricks that never fail to deliver, all these were fiddlesticks to Mima. Fiery and intrusive, she took no time before she neighed to the nearest available stud—good enough reason for a more sturdy character to step aside over the next meeting.

Masinca had a most delicate way to describe how, through a cynical twist of fate, this handsome, even stout young woman, was not quite a wholesome female, owing to some inborn flaw that prevented her from enjoying the benefit of sane, regular intercourse and, most likely, accounted for her morbid bias against the natural course, which made her lose all of what little reasoning she had been left with. When one of her kind happened to take her fancy she would spare no pain or trouble, down to self-humiliation; moreover, her callous parsimony melted like snow in spring and she plunged into unrestrained spending on silk stockings, expensive perfume or long hired coach rides. During the last summer, she had squandered a full four thousand lei in no longer than a month's time to pamper and humour Raşelica Nachmansohn. In fact, she had pilfered the money from a certain Haralambescu as the fellow was sunk in drunken sleep at her place. After all, she didn't mind telling the story herself, as she had no use or meaning for such notions as shame or disgrace. She would knowingly leave the curtains apart when she took her clothes off for the night; nay, when the parish priest came to bless the house on Twelfth Day's Eve she would welcome him with nothing on at all.

And yet, whilst amassing every possible flaw, from twisted tongue to twisted sex to twisted mind, as much frivolous as dangerous, candidly playing at hitching and ditching, Mima could be counted on as a humorous and convivial presence—which could not be said about her younger sister Tita, who was as silly and clumsy as her sister was lively and saucy. Now, if they had anything indeed to share in common it was depravity, deception and defilement—for they were both so intensely filthy, and the more so in hot summer weather, that the offensive odour kept one way apart: they simply smeared and stank up the seat they sat on.

Some childhood illness had left its mark on Tita's mental development, and an early hearing impairment had added up to her hostile, gloomy nature. She had come to be avoided by most, to the point that some of the gamblers complained that she had put an evil spell on them. On the other hand, she was on a par with her sister in terms of never rejecting a "client"; however, she was different in that she would never take her clothes off in full light. With people around, her behaviour almost acquired a mark of distinction, which she certainly had not learnt from her blunt parents: Tita would never frolic around or open her mouth to bad language in the way her sister did.

But their bodily frames and faces were so far apart as to put an abyss between two separate stocks. Large, fleshy, and graceless, definitely prone to obesity, Mima had a snub nose, little green eyes overhung by straight, close eyebrows, her forehead hidden under an outstretch of thick brown hair. On the other hand, Tita was short and slender, with dainty wrists and ankles, narrow shoulders and a head remindful of a noble Phanariot matron, brown, almond-shaped eyes, a long, aquiline nose, and fine well-set lips. If anything, however, their charming voices brought them close: each of a different ring, though both as fluid and crystal-clear, making the music of words sound like murmuring water entwined with the rustle of the breeze in the willows. It may well have been their voices that rose my sympathy as I listened to their sad story. Once more, I had living proof of the dire corruption in the progeny of old, degenerate bloodlines which continue to breed against the wiser Malthusian solution. So much humilitation and pain would be thus spared!

Much of the same exuberant tenderness accompanied the departure of "Mama's Dearest" as had her arrival, while the matron of the house assured me such a perfect friend was something to be met once in a lifetime. I replied I saw no reason why one would look for another. And when Masinca was across the threshold and I was just about to cross it, I felt my sleeve being tugged at from behind. It was Mima. She winked, pointed to my companion and raised a certain finger in a gesture too eloquent to be mistaken. Then she rushed back, with a roar of laughter.

As I came out into the yard, I saw that the Arnoteanus' house carried the same mark of sloppiness as its dwellers. To the back of the original ground-floor building a more recent two-floor structure had been added at an oblique angle, with no plaster on the walls and no windows along the flimsy verandah running along the length of the first floor and into a weird wooden tower patched with tin foil, which sheltered the stairs. This ramshackle extension might well have passed unnoticed in the daytime, but the moonlight lent it an eerie quality of mystery. I had stopped to take a better look, when a lugubrious howl from that direction made me start with horror, as it bore little resemblance with even what you might expect to hear from a hound.

'They've brought the old woman again,' explained Masinca; 'the major's mother, you know.'

Poor creature, it seemed as if God had forgotten to call her back home. It was long past when they could re-member she had lost her mind. They might at least have let her live in one place, rather than tossed her around. Her daughter of the Canta family, a rich Moldavian princess, was a stepsister to the major, whom in fact she had totally repudi-ated; and yet, she would still commit her mother to his care at times, only to take her back after a while. The reason why she did so could be anybody's guess, for the princess herself was no more of a regular, dependable character than the rest of the family, what with her musical background and all. In any case, Maiorică was only too happy to receive his decrepit mother in custody for a few months, just because it was all at the expense of the princess and not, by a long shot, that he might have nurtured the faintest tender feeling for the old woman. Besides, the poor creature was nothing of a burden: for one thing, she was kept away from the busy quarters of the house; for another, she did no harm—in fact she did noth-ing at all, made no speech, most of the time squatted motionless in the corner, at the far end of the bed, like a lifeless dummy. On full moon nights, however, even if the curtains were drawn shut, she would climb down from the bed and creep on all fours, letting out that wailing howl I had heard. In any case, she was no sight for sore eyes—a living spectre, almost a wraith.

So this was what had become of the glorious Sultana Negoianu! You might have thought a ghastly avatar under some evil spell, doomed to outlive to ungodly lengths the once lofty amazon whose prodigality had, in a few years only—which was no mean feat at the time—accomplished to enthral the still separated Principalities[145]. The reason I was acquainted with her past was because that enigmatic, alluring smile of her portraits had once inspired me to inquire into this woman's history—a stormy history, which had brought utter disgrace upon the great family of whom she happened to be the last in line. I was so intent on my investigations, as if some hidden sprite kept prompting me I was going to commit the subject to paper some day.

She had been raised in Geneva and Paris, whence she returned at the age of sixteen, displaying the most eccentric fashion and manners. Her impressive dowry, however, was enough argument for infinite tolerance on the part of Minister of Justice Barbu Arnoteanu as he asked her in marriage. It was a short-lived, turbulent matrimony. Shortly after she had given birth to a son, who would grow into our friend

---

145 Allusion is made to Moldavia and Wallachia, two Romanian provinces to be united in 1959 under the single rule of Prince Alexandru Ioan Cuza.

Maiorică, she eloped with some other swain to Moldavia, where she seduced Jassy as she had Bucharest, while tirelessly winding her hips across ballrooms or haughtily horse-riding with a trail of suitors behind. To win her abandoned husband's consent to divorce, she conceded two of her estates to him and went to marry ex-High Chancellor Iordachi Canta, a Russian prince and unsuccessful candidate to the throne of Moldavia. Predictably, it was an even more fragile bond than the former: to live a life with a jealous, as he was niggardly, spouse in the God-forsaken wilderness around Pandina palace lost amidst ancient forests that lined the river Prut was certainly no desirable perspective for the frolicsome Sultana. Indeed, shortly after giving birth to a daughter, Pulcheria, she sneaked away back to Bucharest, never to return. Another two estates were the price for independence regained—and which, this time, she was determined to defend to the end of her time. And so she lived on, infinitely generous with her wealth as well as her body, nay, insatiably so, to the point that she even had hounds play the part with her. I shall comment no further than hinting to some queer correlation between this paroxystic depravity and her subsequent dementia, of increasingly frequent and intense manifestation. One autumn morning, they say, back in 1857, she was found full naked on the lake shore in Herăstrău Gardens.

Which reminds me: Pirgu had proved not one bit disappointing while insisting on "the true-blood" Arnoteanus for the perfect pool to fish an engaging subject for a novel. And he was the first of our group to cross my path after that memorable evening: on the Boulevard[146], right across from Eforie Street, he had seen me coming and was waiting for me, with both arms stretched forward, hands on top of one-another, palms upward, thumbs outstretched and moving idly[147].

'Keep up the good work, Don Lothario,' he said with a low bow, 'and welcome to the club! I see you're on the prowl spurting your spawn to good use. Oh my, the way you bit the bait on Masinca's hook playing the mellow string, nice and easy on the way in. You little rascal, you cockerel, playing the neighbourhood tomcat, hey? But you're still a novice, my friend, with much ahead to learn yet: you've got to be a stout boar to draw the sows your way. Don't waste your time in the first place, or you'll soon run dry; if you smell a bad bargain, say good riddance and ride on. You know what they say, a ready bull will never miss a cow in heat. And if you see them raise their tail, don't ever step back, push right on like a fiery ram—that's the way to match your season!'

'Funny way to show your gratitude after I made your dream come true with the visit to the Arnoteanus,' I retorted.

'You don't say! You all but got me begging on my knees for six months, remember? And if you finally fell in, was it to my benefit, or yours? You, for one, left with a dam-sel hot on your trail, and the other two rascals got their fat

---

146 Another term for Mogoşoaia Bridge (today's Calea Victoriei), which used to be the main promenade of Bucharest.

147 The gesture suggests a fish, which is the figurative term used in Romanian for a pimp.

share too—I'm sure Pantazi hasn't seen such a pile of dough come his way since his mom's womb spit him out. Anyway, let each and every one enjoy their lucky strike—and yours stands well above all, you're standing right outside the gate of Heaven, my friend!'

My manifest indifference to his hollow rhetoric was not enough to stop him.

'There's someone took a fancy to you, the kind you wouldn't even dream of. Beats me what she saw about you, the deuce only knows, but she's pestering me to bring you within her range.'

I showed no interest whatsoever and assured him I was in no mood to add up to the lot of academics who benefited from doctor Nicu's generosity.

'Aha,' he scoffed, 'no chance, my man, you're running from your own shadow there. You'll get it when you least expect, with the full train of trouble and torture and all. It's all in the Scriptures, says it'll "come in glory" for each and every goat, right?... Believe me, all that precaution is a waste of time. In my humble opinion, the sooner you get the clap, the better: you go for the right cure, no more headaches; it never comes back, you know. Then you can go horsing around all you want. And don't tell me about the other sore, they can fix it too. Listen, if you fear a scratch you'll never get up the tree—and then what's your life harvest going to look like, may I ask?'

'You are perfectly right,' I condescended. 'Good bye.'

'What's the big hurry, is Masinca waiting for you?'

'Later. Now I'm trying to find Paşadia and Pantazi.'

And I was not lying about it: it was three days since they had completely disappeared. Paşadia was less of a concern, he might well have left for the mountains—but what about Pantazi?...

'Well then, if you really want to find them, follow me.'

'Where to?'

'Why, can't you really figure it out? The Arnoteanus', the true-blood Arnoteanus!'

The thing itself was less of a surprise than was the fact that it had been Pantazi's ardent wish to return to that place. What was it that might have drawn him there so irresistibly? Gambling was out of the question, for he wasn't much of a gambler—and had he been one, what would those pathetic stakes be in the face of his vast means?

Women, perhaps? For a whole nine months since I had met him and lived closer to him than anyone else I knew nothing of the slightest relationship he might have had, not the tiniest romantic quirk. At one time our conversation had turned to those puppets that, as the story went, were handled as surrogates for seamen's wives, and he had assured me there was nothing of a tall tale about this abominable perversion: you could buy them ready-made, he said, or you could order for a certain semblance. In Holland they made the crème de la crème, for a handsome price you could get the closest likeness possible to the female frame and texture. The thought had inevitably occurred to me that, among the many large chests piled up in his bedroom, one might be hiding the closest possible likeness of his unfaithful, as she was unforgettable, Wanda.

So, if it was neither gambling nor women, what other reason could possibly make him turn his back on the lush profusion of spring's early blossoms in Bucharest? It seems fate baited me into unravelling this mystery, only to reach her subtle ends.

For my part, I can only be grateful for the challenge. Five weeks' regular attendance at the Arnoteanus' allowed for more insight into the basest depravity of the human soul than a long lifespan devoid of a similar experience. A place of indiscriminate hospitality, wide open round the clock, a conglomerate of establishments from café to inn to gambling house to brothel to madhouse, this den of vice was a sanctuary to the dregs of society: gamblers and drunkards, underdogs and upstarts, stray sheep and black sheep, hopeless losers and watchful sycophants, jailbirds and jail-prones—and then the womenfolk, even more repulsive: all those bedraggled crones, now torpid, now peevish, their shaky hands handling the money and the cards across the green table; or the younger lot, with at least one broken marriage behind, prematurely disfigured and deformed by a history of abortion and disease, forever on the chase for the next mate and forever wary of foul play, in a relentless race of making and shaking and breaking affairs along the way of all flesh. A turpid, rancid haze, filtered through the crinkled pinkish paper lamp shades, lingered in suspension and imbued the scene with every attribute of corruption and decay. Everything around looked weathered, sun-tarnished, mould-stained or moth-eaten, dusty and smoked, chipped or ripped and stripped of the faintest notion of good taste. This all-pervading squalor was even more repulsive to Paşadia than the major's insistence while pestering him with the noble line of the Ar-noteanus—in fact a spurious history before the time of voivode Brâncoveanu, who happened to raise one of his domestics to the title of boyar, thus marking the first record ever in the Arnoteanu descendance down to his father. Poor Maiorică proved an imbecile once more, for if he were to brag about his blue blood, he could have easily had recourse to his mother's branch, which was indeed of genuinely noble descent: an old, uninterrupted Wallachian line of the Craioveşti boyars as far back as the mid-fifteenth century, from Great Ban to Great Ban[148] and matrimony ties with voivodes' kin. An imbecile, no doubt, though a blue-blooded one who, but for his parents' inconsiderate waste, would have feasted on a vast legacy and enjoyed such high offices as Adjutant-General to the Crown and Jockey Vice-President. Deprived of it all, he still had no word of regret, reproach or resentment, and bore the misery of his household—for he couldn't possibly fail to feel it—with muffled bitterness, equally disdainful and defying to either contempt or compassion. On the other hand, he was kind and gentle to the humble—though not as far as his wife Leliwa, a Polish lady of noble crest, whose eyes ran wet with tears at the sight of the slightest pain, always ready to give away the last crumb

---

148 A high official title in medieval Wallachia, similar to a viceroy.

on the table or the coat on her back. To be honest, if they were to be weighed for good and bad, neither of them could be judged to deserve their miserable fate.

The unusually warm welcome I was given from my very first calls at the Arnoteanus' made me feel shy and wary, for it was well above my actual station and means. My suspicion that it was due to some white lie Pirgu had fabricated at my expense proved to be correct eventually: he had spread the rumour that Paşadia and Pantazi were particularly fond of me, the former being my uncle, the latter my godfather. This certainly explained the open-arm reception from the house, the more as our trio's attendance suddenly felt as if the Pactolus[149] trickled some of its boon to the place.

This time, the major had hardly noticed that his mother had been taken away and carried to her Moldavian abode. To my regret, I somehow missed the opportunity to see her. Chance did not fail me altogether though, for the place was far from lacking in eccentric specimens—take this young creature, for instance: a lass that reminded me of those tall, thin, colourless celery stalks that grow out of sandy soil in the dark. And the girl was speechless. Speechless, I

---

149 The Pactolus is a Phrygian river (in today's Turkey) that used to accomodate significant deposits of gold in ancient times. As legend has it, King Midas, who had been granted the ability to change into gold whatever he touched, was not late to feel the drawbacks of this miraculous power (the food he touched also changed to gold), and was permitted to wash it away in the river. At this point, mythological fiction meets with historical fact, in that the Pactolus river provided for the great wealth of King Croesus (6th c. B.C.). The legendary Midas and the historical Croesus have come to be mentioned today in such figures of speech as "the Midas touch", or being "as rich as Croesus".

wondered, because she was deaf too? But then, she must have had a secret sense to replace her auditory faculty, for she started up at the slightest noise around and turned to the spot where it came from. She looked so much like the wax model of that frail, scraggy Prussian princess smiling a wan smile from inside a glass case at Monbijou[150]: the same effete, degenerate, pointed features, the same wicked eyes. A solitary figure in what she perceived as a hostile world, she would run away and hide at the slightest attempt to touch her. When I asked Pirgu about her he told me that Maiorică might well have lain down with one of his daughters while he was drunk, very much like the Biblical Lot[151], which would explain how she came to be born. Although my own speculations did not go that far, it did occur to me, however, that it was just possible for a great-granddaughter and her great-grandmother to have shared the same abode for a while—because, shortly after the old woman had been taken away, the little girl disappeared also.

The high esteem I enjoyed among the Arnoteanus did not spare me the tribute in kind to Mima. My various stratagems to postpone a direct encounter, sometimes fairly clever, sometimes desperately threadbare, could not possibly go on forever. And so it came to pass that one afternoon, when we

---

150 Monbijou was a German Rococo palace in central Berlin. A residence for various members of the court, the palace was heavily damaged in World War II and the ruins were completely levelled in 1959, never to be rebuilt.

151 See the Book of Genesis, chapters 11-14 and 19, in the Hebrew Bible.

were somehow left alone, face to face, I thought I had come to the end of my rope.

She invited me to her room and slipped out of what meagre apparel she had on, as if she were preparing to have a bath. I expected she would ask me to do the same; instead, she only asked my opinion about her naked frame and, with deft gestures, went on to spin her hair, make up her face and dress up. Very soon I was in the street, arm in arm with this dashingly smart doll who looked nothing like the sluttish slattern I had been looking at only minutes before. It was very much like her: at home, a soiled jersey, a frayed skirt and felt slippers on bare feet; yet, when she went out—which she rarely did—she looked spick and span, a little boyish perhaps, always with new gloves, well-stretched stockings and glossy patent-leather shoes. And always in a hackney carriage, the best that money could hire.

This time, however, she chose to walk in my company. A lingering stroll it was, with deliberate detours while she kept on chattering with no apparent coherence, constantly changing the subject and mixing it all up in a perfectly hollow monologue. And so we came up in front of Paşadia's house, which seemed to radiate a magic light against the dusky evening. She stood there with a long, dreamy gaze and inquired in detail about the interior, the furniture, the domestics—a rainfall of questions the meaning of which I failed to grasp till the last one fell on me like a hammer: how would I take her for my auntie? Her mind was stuck on Paşadia, the man she wanted in wedlock to the best of her purposes.

Had we been on friendly terms at that time, like we came to be later, I would have told her bluntly to shake it off her mind. I knew Paşadia only too well, as I had come to know Pantazi: the former, an uncompromising snob fettered by infantile prejudice; the latter, a shrewd entrepreneur when it came to the push, no less adroit in business proceedings than his usurer uncle or his expert father. No, definitely not. Paşadia would never make such a step—not with Mima, in any case: he found her boring, tedious, nothing to his taste. His sympathies went with Tita, whose nature was more like his own: very much like those ruthless raptors which, even when fatally wounded, with broken wings, will dash one last time at the inimical victor.

I had, for a while, shared in Paşadia's opinion about Mima, only to change my mind soon: a lunatic she was, no doubt about that, more wicked, dirty and treacherous than what Masinca had decried her to be; yet agreeable and congenial, sweet and seductive like sin incarnate, lithe and sprightly like flames or ripples. Now overwhelmed by desperate melancholy, the next minute hysterically exultant; now drab and dismal, then coming alive with a sudden spark of free, lofty spirit in her countenance; sometimes she bore herself like a boiled rag, bent from the loins, her eyes narrow, dimmed slits on a pale, faint face—only to swiftly rise to an upright poise, brisk and blooming, moist lips and eyes glistening like dew. A protean presence she was, and even her miserable affliction added up to her appeal, forever to be desired and never to be possessed, much like those vapoury fairies, creatures born of wind and water, intangible to the embrace of mortals. Indeed, those two rascals had definitely

not paid too high a price—one his honour, the other his life—
for the privilege of having known her...

...and so she was insisting on my service to fulfil her
design.

I promised to do all that stood in my power, yet advised her that Paşadia was far more sensitive to Pirgu's influence rather than mine. I noticed her nose screwing up in distaste behind the blue beaded net veil. I knew something had
happened between her and Gore, to neither's eventual content. When they met face to face they played the best of
friends: she would dance before him and sing, 'Master Gore,
handsome man, time and time and time again', while he
bowed low, his hand to his heart, calling her Sweet Princess,
Your Highness, Your Majesty: he would be blessed, he said,
to be the carpet that rested her dainty feet; he would deed
himself in slavery to her, after the Ottoman fashion—and the
like. Backstage, there was but smearing and slander on both
sides: she called him a rogue and a villain and said she
wished he ended up in a madhouse or a dungeon, while he
summoned the fiercest curses upon her, calling her a slut and
a slattern and a tramp and a trollop, and prayed the Lord
would keep his legs nimble enough to get to waltz on her
tomb.

'Well,' conceded Mima, 'after all, I may as well humour Pirgu, if I have to.' This was not so easy though, for
Gore had lately ceased to patronise the Arnoteanus' establishment. He had struck a most fortunate bargain with his

share of the legacy as he managed to sell it away to some brother-in-law for almost double the price he had hoped for, which made his life take a sharp turn. The year of the monkey had got the better of him—which could fairly be said about myself too, as I had switched from carefully avoiding him to sheepishly following in his steps.

A burlesque comedy it was. The minute I met with him, I would feign haste, and my answer to his natural curiosity as to where I was headed was invariable: 'The Arnoteanus' of course, the true-blood Arnoteanus!'

I managed to annoy him eventually: 'There you go again,' he exploded, 'forever harping on the same string! Will you spare me... *Vous devenez agassant avec vos Arnoteano.*[152] Sod them! *Voyons, il faut être serieux!*'[153]

Not for the world would he give up his unfathomable treasure of juicy expletives—apart from which, however, he only blabbered in French now, as loudly as no passing ear should miss it. While walking by his side, I would always cross the street away from him if I saw a lady approaching, and if I happened to know her I would vanish into the nearest gangway or courtyard. As for him, he made a theatrical step back to let her pass and cried out, '*Regardez, mon cher, quelle jolie femme, comme elle est jolie, elle est jolie comme tout!*'[154] When the lady was out of sight I showed my face

---

152 (French) You are becoming a pest with your Arnoteanus.

153 (French) Come on, let's be serious!

154 (French) Look, my dear, what a lovely woman, she's so lovely, lovely as can be!

again. He would turn to me with an offended mien: '*Mais, mon pauvre ami, ne soyez pas idiot; vous êtes bête comme vos pieds!*'[155]

With that, he would leave me behind and make a few bow-legged steps ahead; then he stopped, put on his monocle and pointed his cane at the rooftops pretending to be keenly observing something. Finally he turned around, sniffing at me and shrugging his shoulders: '*Mais voyons, voyons*[156].' A crazy shopping spree followed inevitably, to order furniture for the house he intended to build for himself in Romanian traditional style, then at the flea market for icons, which he piled up indiscriminately: in just a few days, an entire wall of the hotel room on Victoria Road where he had moved in lately had been covered with sloppy Virgins and scrawny saints, amongst which one could not miss a bluish-brown, fierce-looking St Haralambie towering over the defeated Plague, fettered at his feet. Yet this was nothing compared to something else which, had I cared for him in all honesty, should have raised my worries: unbelievably, Pirgu went about buying books! My jaw literally dropped when I met him once carrying four nicely bound volumes under his armpit, with the name of Montaigne[157] on the covers!

---

155 (French) My dear fellow, don't be an idiot; you are as stupid as a goose!

156 (French) Literally: Let's see. In this context, esp. when repeated, approx.: Oh, come on, let's be reasonable.

157 Michel Eyquem de Montaigne (1533-1592) was a French statesman and one of the most influential authors of the Renaissance age, best known for his volume of essays (Essais), inspired by his studies of the classics, notably Plutarch.

'Montaigne?!' I exclaimed. 'What's biting you, for God's sake?'

'Well, you know,' he replied with a sheepish grin, 'Montaigne is nice after all, he's got his good side…'

It was his way to make an opinion in most conversations with his newly acquired friends, distinguished barristers or university fellows, figures of reputed name and fame. He had turned his back on his old disgraceful company altogether, pretending he didn't even know them, and it was a unique treat for me to see Pirgu in his favourite bistro, toward midnight, having a delicate snack in the eyes of the scum from all across Bucharest, piled up round the tables to watch him. Questions were heard in mock-curiosity: 'Hey mate, who might that bloke be?' And the answer followed in line: 'He's English; you may as well cuss him, he won't get none of it.' And curse him they did, from the doorway, behind the pillars or from under the tables, and they called out, 'Gore, Gorică!'—all to no visible effect. In ostensibly candid ignorance of their assault, Gore would eat and drink unruffled, then went on to relish expensive cigarettes, all the more as it was often at their own expense.

Though he had somehow managed to get admission cards to two illustrious clubs, Pirgu continued to patronise his regular gambling den where he could freely brag about his big money—he always carried it all upon him—and also look down his nose at Pașadia, with whom he had been at odds for some time. At some point during mutual teasing and nagging, it so happened that Pașadia cleared him out of a handsome stake. Instead of sensibly standing up and leaving to meet his dear friends, prospective statesmen, and listen to them discussing Bergson[158] and the Hague Conference[159], Pirgu set his jaw to make up for the loss. Paşadia's biting indifference and the humiliating smirks and spurns from those he had offended boggled his mind to the point that he made a mess of the play and lost everything—indeed, a fortune. In the early hours Paşadia, who had raked in the bulk of the stakes, stood up to leave and left Pirgu to the rookies to shake him free of the last crumbs. As he returned home that morning, more desolate than his own pockets, his angry eyes fell on poor St Haralambie whom he blamed for having cast a spell on him; he snatched the icon off the hook and whirled it out of the window and into the hotel patio. Now, I don't know if our ungodly times had ever recorded the miracle of an icon landing from heaven—there is, however, another miracle I confess I had least expected—in fact, it somewhat annoyed me: I had never imagined a miser like Gore to be so pliant and resilient. In short, no later than the next evening, reconciled with Paşadia, and maybe with his own fate, Gore turned up at the Arnoteanus', perfectly composed and ready for the next battle.

As Pantazi and I called at the said place toward noon one day, we came across an unfamiliar presence: a damsel, seated with one leg bent to her chest, the bare foot resting on the chair, was darning a sock while humming softly to her-

---

158 Henri Bergson (1859-1941), French philosopher, supporter of experience and intuition over rationalism and science.

159 The First Hague Conference (1899) and the Second Hague Conference (1907) negotiated formal statements of the laws of war and war crimes in the context of international law.

self. As we entered she raised her eyes and blushed up to her ears. I saw Pantazi go pale as death in an instant; he took his hand to his heart and whispered feebly: 'My God, what an incredible resemblance!'

It was thus that we made the acquaintance of Miss Ilinca Arnoteanu. It had been brought to our knowledge that there was one more lass in the family, the youngest of three, who had been raised from the cradle by a sister of the major's wife's from Piatra Neamț, a well-off widow with no progeny of her own. Now barely sixteen, Ilinca had spent the spring of her life pampered by the serenity of that blissful countryside with a magic skyline, which must have reminded the noble knights to whom the place owes its name of their sweet native Swabia[160]. Mima had nicknamed her 'new' sister *Fräulein*, which was not far from a fair description, considering both the place where she came from and her appearance. The mild sun of Moldavia had spared the uncanny ashen blondness of her braids and her nacre-pale skin. I imagined her naked in the dark, she must have been luminous there. Both parents were perfectly proud of her: Elvira could not help praising her beauty—Maiorică, her diligence. Without the slightest constraint, Ilinca had always come in first in class, and now she was preparing for compact graduation of two consecutive school years. Coincidentally, she bore the same name as that wise and highly educated ancestor of hers, a princess in the Negoianu bloodline, daughter to Voivode Petrașcu; and again, it was common knowledge that the pen

160 Swabia (German: Schwaben) is a historic region in SW Germany – hence the connection with the toponym Piatra Neamț or Piatra Neamțului (German, literally, the German's Stone).

of Enache II, himself an Arnoteanu, had marked the dawn of the renaissance of Romanian letters. Indeed, Ilinca was glued to her books all day, lying on the bed while shyly covering her feet, as if ashamed of their tiny size. She lacked the sprightliness one would expect at her age: her conduct was strange to laughter and jest, and the stern look that hardened her still childish features spelt definite rejection of what she saw going on around her.

I had accepted to help her with a few subjects of which she felt she did not have a firm grasp. In the meantime, while conversing about this and that, I was impressed by her sound, crystal-clear reasoning. When I once confessed to her I had seldom met someone who would study like she did, just for their own pleasure, she observed that, besides the pleasure she took in her studies, she also did it to the practical purpose of acquiring a profession. Why, was she not going to be rich? After all, it was known for a fact that she was the single in-heritor to her aunt, whose consistent pension added up an annual double in interest. True, but wealth could be lost at any moment; and then, wealth did not stand in the way of profes-sional accomplishment—quite the opposite, in fact. What, with her name?!... Yes, why not? There is no shame in pursu-ing a trade; work only brings honour and dignity to one's ex-istence. As for her name, it would serve her all the better as a school teacher—which was what she wanted to become; it would be a reason for higher appreciation and respect. To gain and be worthy of respect was her most ardent wish. As for her name, she was perfectly aware what it weighed and what she owed it. That name still loomed large, it was some-thing she had discovered before even being told about its prestige: at some point during an examination, a presumptuous inspector was surprised by the astute answers of this little schoolgirl, Arnoteanu Ilinca, and asked if she happened to belong in the "historic" Arnoteanu family. When it was confirmed to him, he immediately called her "young lady" and, in flattering words, he held her up as an example worthy to follow. Again, when her aunt took her on visits to Madam Elena Cuza[161], why would she always be seated by the host's side, if not because she was a "true-blood" Arnoteanu? Indeed, she was determined to bear in all dignity the noble name of a distinguished line of dignitaries, scholars and founders of establishments—a name that her sisters had done enough to discredit.

Ah, the sisters! The genuine compassion she felt for them could not hinder the sharp critical judgment she had of them. Why had they not struggled to get the better of their impulses and instincts, like she had?... And so I learnt that, behind her cold, dispassionate appearance, as of an iced blancmange, the hot blood of her grandmother had bitterly tried and ruffled her blooming senses from early girlhood: she had sailed through savagely stormy nights when her crude flesh was burning with desire; she had been sick, indeed on the verge of insanity, yet she held tight and would not for the world yield to dishonour...

Now, probably sensing her confession had gone too far, she veered from the subject with awkward haste and asked my opinion on her capacity to pass the two exams that confronted her. Neither, I said in a perfectly detached and

---

161 Elena Cuza was the wife of Prince Alexandru Ioan Cuza, the ruler who united the Romanian Principalities of Wallachia and Moldova in 1859.

assured tone, and explained that she would be in wedlock before the first, and out of the country before the second.

For it had all been arranged. The moment he saw Ilinca, Pantazi was utterly struck by her resemblance with his Wanda of yore, which instantly sparked and rekindled the old flame in him. This weird passion of his was nothing like the pinnacle of gradual infatuation, but rather a ravaging outburst which he had no intention to resist—on the contrary, he let it consume him with perverse, masochistic delight. He kept thinking of the girl all the time, spoke of nothing but her, and engaged me to talk to him about her—anything, good or bad, only let it be about her. And he applied himself to drinking— not more than usual, it would have hardly been possible; the difference was, however, he got so easily drunk this time. Dead-drunk, that is—so much so that I had to carry him home on my back twice. He would ask me to escort him on nightly expeditions round the Arnoteanus' estate, and he thrilled as he approached the window behind which his dearest beloved slept. He entrusted me with all of the heartfelt beautiful things he wished he had told her and never could, for in her presence his speech would falter and he shied away, timorous of even looking her in the eye. But as I was the sole recipient of his secret torment, his peculiar behaviour passed unnoticed amidst the boiling turmoil at the Arnoteanu establishment. And Pantazi would never have crossed the line unless, driven by the most candidly friendly feelings I had for both of them, I had made up my mind to unite them in marriage.

One evening, sober and clear in the head, he launched in his usual tirade about how desperately much he loved her. I seized the chance and told him forthright that I had my doubts, that it was all in his mind perhaps; for had it been true, he would at least have been engaged by then. What was he waiting for, why not go ahead and ask her hand in marriage? It seemed as if he was blind to the miracle of meeting his dream love incarnate once more, thirty years later, this time an ideal avatar, perfectly worthy of him. Had his mind been set on it, he would not for a moment have hesitated to lay all his wealth at the feet of this adorable lass who had risen against the twilight of his life like the full moon shining its pearly salute to the setting sun. Then again, had he thought for a minute that Ilinca might come to belong to someone else—and soon? Were not her beauty, her name and her capital more than enough assets for a host of suitors to queue up at her door?

My last words were like a cold shower to Pantazi, who had until then listened as if in a trance, now and then parroting my words in a dreamlike mumble. I had finally plucked the string of jealousy in his heart, that impish impulse, so deeply embedded in human nature, that makes it less painful to lose something or somebody altogether than for someone else to have it in your place—a woman all the more so. I had thus won Ilinca's case. The next day, I had to stand up for his case against her. In all good faith, I explained to her the benefits she and her folks would enjoy from marrying my friend. She listened patiently, as unemotional as ever, and did not even ask me for some time to think it over—instead, she said she would readily accept if my description of his wealth proved to be at least half true. And since agreement from her parents and her aunt was the least of a problem, the road seemed to be clear, with nothing to stand in the way. But to anticipate a smooth, untroubled development was to ignore Pirgu's existence in the plot.

Since he had materialised again at the Arnoteanus' he seemed to have run into a frenzy, rushing in and out of every door in the house, to the effect that you might say there were more than one Gorică. When he fed the establishment with gamblers he brought them wholesale, in herds. And he took a sudden fancy to Maiorică—he would not stop pampering him, kissing him, sticking his tongue into the poor fellow's mouth. They would often leave together at dusk and return toward midnight, each time more jovial and chirpy. His mind was fully set on Maiorică, he talked to us about little else than his admiration for him—oh, if only we knew what a phi-landerer he could be: he had turned the head of a fifteen-year-old damsel, such a sweet lass she was, and a virgin too. And he nudged Pantazi, who would not raise his eyes while his cheeks changed colour, to be no less of a ram as long as God had not yet spared him from temptation, like Pașadia. Soon enough, Maiorică had to atone painfully for his all-to-easy seduction; and it was the same Gore who entrusted him to Dr. Nicu's care.

Nevertheless, this was but petty villainy compared with what had been secretly conspired, all in parallel with the aforesaid hush arrangements for Ilinca's wedding. I learnt it from Pirgu himself, over a glass of cheap grape brandy out-side the market place, one early morning. I did not realise at first if it was the hangover after a whole night's orgy or he was just trifling with me, as I had so far been of opinion that such things could only come out of soap operas. I had, it seems, definitely forgotten that we lived at the Gates of the Orient. As he deemed the fair sex as mere commodity, he could not but take Ilinca for a princely prize, whereupon he had readily started to weave the plot, taking advantage of the propitious circumstances. All the big money we had seen flowing through the Arnoteanus' hands since we had started to patronise their establishment had sunk in their insatiable, prodigal extravagance; ergo, they found themselves close to their lowest ebb, while Paşadia was drowning in lucky strikes at the green table and had lost count of his gains. Pirgu, a sly fox when it came to pandering, had reckoned he could put these opposites to good use and somehow talked Madam Elvira into selling away her daughter, and Paşadia into buying her for a huge price, as monstrously gross as the bargain itself, of which he was to derive the lion's share.

And so I came to understand the design of the hasty arrangement that had been made to visit the religious establishments round the city: we were to spend the night at a certain nunnery, where they would intoxicate Ilinca with a glass or two and then leave her alone in Paşadia's company. Once I had learnt of such a mean scheme, it would have been all too easy for me to dismantle and dissolve it into silence and oblivion, had it not been for the fact that Pirgu met Pantazi only minutes after he had parted with me and confided to him the same story as he had to me. I was grateful to Almighty Providence for somehow keeping me away from what came to happen a few hours later at the Arnoteanus', where Paşadia had invited Pantazi for lunch. Alone in the salon, still over appetizers, they suddenly got entangled in the most desperate fracas, inconsiderate of the mess they made while toppling chairs and breaking glassware and crockery. One could easily imagine the faces of those who ran to the racket, only to watch Paşadia and Pantazi slapping, punching and kicking each-other to the best of their means, rolling across the floor, taking turns at riding on top of the other. In the end, Pantazi looked the most disheveled and mangled suitor to have ever asked a girl's hand, true-blood Arnoteanu or not.

The news of the mayhem was brought to me by a still befuddled Pirgu, shortly after I had received a message from each of the two belligerents, each asking me to serve as his witness in an armed duel, and to find a second witness.

To prevent the encounter was easier than I would have thought. With his back turned on the world, Paşadia was still extremely sensitive to public opinion, and this was the string I plucked as I told him how his reputation of a gentleman would be irreparably shattered when this affair—which could be anything but honourable—fell prey to the talk of the town. And I was not wrong, as Ilinca was not wrong to follow my advice and ask him to decline the duel, as a wedding token. I was thinking, beyond my personal annoyance, that Paşadia's hand might be as unfortunately lucky as to ruin the poor girl's fortune. In the meantime, she had written to her aunt from Moldova and invited her to come over. Instead of one, however, there were two who arrived. The large white-and-red pennant had been removed from the roof of the Pandina palace as Princess Pulcheria left for Bucharest with her retinue of, as she called them, "clean beasts"—a parrot, two dogs and three cats—and "unclean beasts"—a French maid, an Italian domestic, a gypsy cook and two fiddlers, one Czech and one German. Two days before, Dospinescu, her old bailiff, had emptied four large hotel rooms to accommodate them for her respectable bulk of travel accoutrements; he had also leased two Bösendorfers[162] and employed two hackney coachmen, one for the daytime and one for the night.

High-class extravagancy, one might say. But indeed the lady deserved pardon for vanities even greater than that, for she was, after all, a genuine artist. Her music salon in Paris and, before all else, that breed of brilliant musicians, either composers or virtuoso performers, who had stepped into the limelight under her consummate guidance, had saved the name of Princess Canta from oblivion and into the front lines of the late-nineteenth-century history of music.

I was to learn that she had been Pantazi's earliest friend. Back in 1863, as Justice Canta came to Bucharest to settle some cause, he and his daughter were hosted for several months by Lady Smaranda at her residence, where the rank and fashion of the time would line up to listen to little Pulcheria playing the piano. The girl was the same age as ***, and they lived there together, very much like brother and sister. They both cherished the memory of those days, and remembered each-other as the one-time tallish, swarthy brunette, bold and confident, and the blond boy, short, frail, diffident and reserved. After his departure from the country, she had been the only person from our society with whom he had entertained contact: they wrote to each-other, they met in Milan, Bayreuth, Paris. Now he had felt it his duty to let her know without delay that he had decided to marry his niece.

As he had gone to Milcov to welcome her, she had barely recognised him and, surprised by his new appearance, was delighted to hear the story that had led him to change his

---

162 A piano brand of Austrian make.

name. Also, she was eager to meet Ilinca. The long interview between aunt and niece had an unexpected result: perfectly charmed by the young lady, the princess—who had also had a short, infertile marriage to a certain Canta from a different branch—vowed to Ilinca that she would legally adopt her as her daughter.

One piece of news delighted me as much as the next sank my spirits. To please the other aunt of hers, Ilinca agreed to postpone the wedding till after May, the Month of Mary[163]—a delay of almost three weeks which visibly discontented Pantazi, who became melancholy and worried.

One evening he insisted that we should have supper at his place, just the two of us. We left the house at a late hour and mounted a carriage which seemed to be a fortuitous appearance at the corner of the street, but soon proved to have been waiting for Pantazi as, with no indication from him, the coachman drove us through streets unknown to me and out of town. Such outings were not new to me: toward the autumn of the past year we had often been trotted to the nearby countryside at night, where we would climb some hillock to contemplate Fomalhaut[164] just above the horizon. On that night, however, there were neither stars nor moon, the sky was overcast and there was a milky light that brought into sight almost all shapes around, and the trees even seemed to be lit from the inside. At a bend of the road Pantazi ordered the

---

163 In the Catholic faith, the month of May is dedicated to the Virgin Mary, with special devotions to the Mother of God. A popular superstition among Christians advises against weddings in May.

164 Fomalhaut is the brightest star in the constellation Piscis Austrinus.

coachman to halt, invited me to step down and follow him. A roofless ruined structure was grinning farther away.

'The Devil's Inn,' said Pantazi. There are more like this across Ilfov County[165], each sunken in its own sinister history populated with brigands and ghosts. In this one here I joined a carousal party once, which ran all through the night, under the light of torches.'

'How odd,' he murmured in a muffled voice, 'the beans have shown nothing but a death omen.'

I quenched my indignation at such stupid superstitions coming from a man like him, and made a quick calculation of how many days were left to the end of the month. I had already lodged the documents for the wedding, and the princess's solicitor was hasting along with the adoption papers. The growing indifference affected by Ilinca as to all these preparations had come to annoy me as much as her insolent speech and conduct towards both strangers and her own kinsfolk. I suspected sheer hypocrisy when, with that peculiar smile reminiscent of her grandmother's portraits, she told me that, if all else failed, she would return to Piatra Neamț with no regret other than for a lost schoolyear. She had refused all jewellery from Pantazi, for what, she said, could it be compared with what she had inherited from lady Smaranda? All she had asked for was a photographic camera. It was, eventually, the instrument which sealed her fate. One morning, as she saw a little girl in droll apparel waiting in the milkmaid's "phaeton", she requested that the poor girl be brought over to take her photograph. Incidentally, the girl was just recovering

---

165 A county which comprised Bucharest.

from scarlet fever, and so the germs easily found their way to Ilinca. A slight affliction at first, which she thought would soon pass of itself, the disease suddenly broke out so fiercely that all the doctors in Bucharest, plus another one who was hastily brought from Vienna, had to admit to their defeat, for all the promise of a million to him who would save her. And this was the end of Ilinca.

On the very morning of her demise, a short note from Pantazi was asking me to see to the funeral procedures. Definitely, he had no idea he was requesting something beyond my powers. I needed someone to help me out, and there was no one I knew who could do it better than Pirgu. I went out to find him, but it proved no easy feat. From Dușumea to Vitan to Geagoga to Obor[166], hopping off one carriage and on to the next, I searched all his regular dens at least once, all to no eventual avail. Of all whom I asked about his whereabouts, only Haralambescu had seen him at Moși[167] the last evening, drunk as a pig, in the company of a barefooted slut far-gone with child. Around two o'clock after noon I resigned myself to the thought that I was to do it all by myself. Before I proceeded on the melancholy mission, however, I remembered that nothing had touched my palate since the night before and, as I felt an inkling of fatigue creeping through my legs, I

166 Old names of various Bucharest districts.

167 The name of a popular fun fair in Bucharest in the early- and mid-1900s.

called at Capşa's[168] for a cup of coffee and a *kirsch*[169]. And there he was, purple in the face with rage, cursing like a sailor—Pirgu in the flesh!

'I imagined I'd find you in loftier spirits after last night's exploit,' I said to him. He put on a wide grin:

'*Di granda*[170] it was, I tell you, she almost delivered in my lap!' And, while he was leisurely sipping my coffee and my *kirsch*, I told him the story. I needed not even ask him to involve himself in the funeral. I gave him carte blanche and, indeed, had no reason for regret. On the third day, the most resplendent day ever for a month of May, Ilinca was taken to her last resting place in full splendour, like a Byzantine empress, bathed in a profusion of flowers. What struck me about the funeral was neither the despondency, presumably also poisoned with remorse, of the aunt from Piatra, nor the parents' twofold grief for losing a daughter and, with her, the last promise of a milder fortune, nor the unconcealed, impudent satisfaction of the two sisters, jealous and hateful of the deceased as she had been disdainful of them; what really struck and even worried me was the absence of Pantazi. Pirgu had not yet finished his eulogy when I left and hurried back into town, obsessed with the thought that Pantazi might have taken his own life. But as I passed by the windows of the French bistro I saw him through the open blinds, seated at his

---

168 A fashionable bistro and restaurant on Victoria Road (then Podul Mogoşoaiei) in the centre of Bucharest.

169 Cherry brandy (short for German Kirschwasser).

170 Italian for "great", "excellent", "fabulous".

reserved table in the far corner, eating and drinking heartily, perfectly composed. From that day on, he never set foot again in the Arnoteanus' house and never mentioned Ilinca again, as if she had never been...

*

...it was three months since Pantazi and I had resumed our habits of the last year, with late suppers till after midnight, followed by timeless strolls through anonymous slums and deserted alleys, all the way into the morning light. We listened to the voice of autumn whisper in the rich foliage, which now looked deep and heavy like never before in the mesmeric twilight of fabulous sunsets, as if time itself were lingering in its pace. It so happened that, one of those days, I fell asleep under the setting sun, and had the most beautiful dream of my life.

My dream was about an old court where, in the chapel of sinful passions, the three Superiors of the halcyon brotherhood were serving their last Vespers, a silent service of the Vespers into the beyond. Dressed up in their tall cloaks, broadswords hanging from our hips and large crosses crossing our chests, all garbed and braided and plumed in a pageant of golden and green, green and golden, save for the scarlet of the scabbards, we were standing in wait for the blessed redemption of our exile on earth. With a gentle jingle, an unseen bell heralded that the divine grace had perched upon us.

Redeemed through pride, we were to regain our lofty thrones. From above the pews, unseen squires had lowered the escutcheoned standards, and the seven candles in the altar went out one by one. A bridge was cast westwards and the three of us proceeded along it, passing huge celestial vaults arched over the giant void. Ahead of us went Pirgu in motley harlequin's attire, hopping and dancing as he walked backwards, his face a display of grotesque grimaces while waving a black kerchief. And so we melted into the twilight of the setting sun...

A few days later, still under the impression of the dream, I called at the bistro for the latest news, only to learn that Paşadia had died. His departure did not go unnoticed, though not in itself as much as in the way it happened. Hardly a social presence of late, Paşadia had gone to live with Raşelica Nachmansohn. The woman was notorious for her frantic passion for a certain carnal practice which Gorică had aptly described as he called her a leech. A victim of his own design, Paşadia was not long to give out under her ruthless assaults when, eventually, the blood gushed with the last spurt of manly vigour and the heart stopped ticking. A worthy descendant of her glorious forebear Judith[171], Raşelica did not lose her head: perfectly self-possessed, she disentangled her hair from the dead man's still warm grip, then dressed up neatly and went to ask the police commissioner to undertake the necessary arrangements to clear the place of the corpse—which was accomplished with the discreet assent

---

171 See the Book of Judith in the Old Testament of the Bible.

of the higher ranks. After all, to what avail would it have been to spread the fire? And so it came that, at early dawn as usual, Paşadia made his last homecoming. Without delay I hurried to the dismal place, only to see a plume of smoke as I approached, raising above the trees of the flowerless garden. The faithful hand had fulfilled its duty. In his bitter hatred, the man had managed to put into effect the most perversely refined of crimes. I deplored the loss of a great work, though not that of their author.

Paşadia died at the crest of his life; venom, vigil and vice had consumed his body, only to crumble in limp impotence at the gate of his spirit, which sparkled like a morning star through frigid frosty nights, crystal-clear to the very end. All the more fortunate was he to have been spared the ordeal of the war[172] and, with it, the experience of poverty once more, the more humiliating this time as it would have come in his late years. Even more painful, perhaps, would have been for him to see how Pirgu disproved his somber predictions—to see Pirgu a multimillionaire, married with a handsome dowry and then divorced for handsome key money; to see Pirgu climb from prefect to Parliament representative to senator to plenipotentiary, presiding over a subcommission for intellectual cooperation with the League of Nations and accommodating his foreign confreres, who came to Romania on charity missions or to make some "enquiry", in his ancient castle in Ardeal, where he treated them with sumptuous hospitality.

---

172 World War I, which Romania joined in 1916.

I did not see Paşadia dead. His place was being sealed when I arrived, and, following his wish, Iancu Mitan had hurried to take his corpse away, somewhere outside Bucharest—"to the mountains", maybe…

Having finally managed to sell away the last of his properties, the petty shop near Bărăţia, Pantazi had ridded himself of the last bond that held him in place. On the eve of his departure we dined together at the bistro in Covaci Street. Not far from our table, more dazzling and more carefree as ever, Raşelica showed off her new fiancé, a dumpy, stumpy, froggy-looking fellow with bulging eyes. Once more, the fiddlers played the sensual, sad waltz for which Pantazi had a soft spot, that languid sway that carried a wavering, wistful, infinitely woeful key to leave a dolorous mark on any listening ear. The rumour in the room fell into dead silence as the deep magic of the melody went gliding across the bridged cords of the fiddles. Sinking to lingering lower tones, gently subdued to the sound of painful tenderness and chagrin, the music overflowed with wistful redolence of agonising fantasy, fading away in tardy, hopeless desire.

Pantazi wiped his moist eyes.

We spent the whole night ambling around the city, only to find ourselves, at dawn, in the same flower market by the Old Court. Our attention was caught by a feeble flickering light near the fence of the green-steepled church. Some anonymous hand had lit a candle at the head of a dead woman who lay in all decency on a mat. Had I not been told, I would never have thought it was Pena Corcoduşa. How could I ever have recognized the fearful Fury of the last year in the tender features of that gentle face? Those ashy lips had frozen in a smile which spelt infinite fondness. The woman who had gone insane with love seemed to have died a mercifully happy death. God willing, at that last split-moment which opened the gate into eternity, her sweet prince had come to meet her, the proud cavalier whose earthly avatar had garnered the glory of two imperial crowns.

On that same evening I was on my way to accompany a stranger to the country border: a clean-shaven gentleman with short whiskers, smartly dressed in travel attire. We were both sitting there, face to face, in the dining car of the train, while words were locked somewhere at the back of our minds. Night had fallen fast outside. And I came to remember the man who was no longer there, the man I had felt to be an age-old friend, if not my very alter-ego, only when Pantazi asked me what we might like to drink.

Made in the USA
Middletown, DE
05 March 2015